Between Two Worlds

A Novel

Between Two Worlds

A Novel

LeAnne Hardy

Kregel
Publications

Between Two Worlds

Published by Kregel Publications, a division of Kregel, Inc., P.O. Box 2607, Grand Rapids, MI 49501.

This story is fiction. The characters are the product of the author's imagination and are not intended to represent any actual individuals.

Library of Congress Cataloging-in-Publication Data
Hardy, LeAnne.
Between two worlds / by LeAnne Hardy.
     p. cm.
     [1. Missionaries—Fiction. 2. High schools—Fiction.
3. Schools—Fiction. 4. Christian Life—Fiction.] I. Title.
PZ7.H22143 Be 2003
[Fic]—dc21
                                          2003001779

ISBN 0-8254-2793-2

Printed in the United States of America

03 04 05 06 07 / 5 4 3 2 1

Para Érika,
minha Campo Grandense

Chapter 1

"VARIG flight 27 for Miami with a stop in São Paulo now departing from Gate 2." The breathy voice on the intercom might as well have been a hideous cackle, the way Cristina Larson's stomach clutched. She did not want to get on that plane.

"*Não!*" Márcia drew out the Portuguese word in a long moan. She embraced Cristina, and soon both girls were sobbing. "A year is so long! You've got to write to me. All the time. Promise?"

Cristina nodded and groped for a tissue in her pocket.

"Tell me all about your birthday," Márcia continued. "It will be wonderful having your *quinze anos* in America!"

Cristina wasn't at all sure that was true. Her Brazilian friend probably imagined that Rum River, Minnesota, was right next door to Disney World. Why did their year in the States have to be now? Why couldn't it be last year or next year—any time but the year of her fifteenth birthday?

"Come on, Cristina. I want to hug Márcia, too, and we have to go." Cristina's older sister, Bete, stood by her side.

Márcia gave Cristina another squeeze and kissed her on both cheeks, then she kissed Cristina's right cheek one more time. "For luck," she whispered. They both knew what kind of luck she had in mind.

Everyone hugged and talked at once. So many last minute things needed to be said, and not enough time was left to take turns. How Cristina wished she could stay! She hated good-byes, hated pulling up roots and going to America. It might be "home" for her parents, but western Brazil was the only home Cristina wanted.

Márcia's mother dabbed at her eyes with a tissue and gave Cristina an extra kiss for romantic luck as well. Cristina giggled despite her tears. She was sure *Tia* Dalva had no idea that the "luck" Cristina hoped for was the tall handsome son at her side.

Vicente's dark eyes met Cristina's, and he put his strong arms around her. Then he took her shoulders firmly and kissed her on both cheeks. Her skin tingled, and for a brief moment Cristina wondered how long she could get away with not washing her face. *Tio* Zé and Cristina's father hugged and slapped each other soundly on the back as they said their own farewells.

The voice on the intercom repeated the boarding call. Cristina picked up her carry-on bag. It was heavy with all the treasures she couldn't force into her suitcase, but couldn't bear to leave behind. Shuffling through the gate after Bete, Cristina stopped every few steps and looked back at her friends. The black tarmac reflected the heat of the Brazilian sun. Halfway to the plane, she stopped once more and looked back at the terminal. It seemed like she had done this a hundred times before. It never got any easier. Vicente had his arm around Márcia who rested her dark, curly head on her brother's shoulder and waved a last farewell.

"I hate good-byes." Cristina clenched her teeth and started up the steps to the plane.

❄ ❄ ❄

The corridor of Rum River High School was noisy and crowded with strangers.

"What are you looking at?" The girl at the next locker glared at Cristina. Cristina snapped her mouth shut to keep from answering back and jerked her eyes away from the girl's tight neon outfit. Her cheeks felt hot, and she knew they were as bright as the other girl's top. The girl slammed her locker and swept away.

"If she doesn't want to be looked at, she shouldn't dress like that!" Cristina muttered. She rubbed her nose and shook her head at the stale smell of tobacco the girl had left behind. Then a horrible thought scratched at Cristina's mind. She glanced down at her outfit and looked anxiously around the corridor.

Most of her fellow students were dressed in T-shirts and jeans. Some were wrinkled; some merely limp. Cristina wondered if Americans had ever heard of ironing. Here and there one or two students wore loud, tight outfits.

Evidently it was some American idea of *bacana*—"cool"

or whatever the "in" word here was. But Cristina wasn't impressed. She and Bete had stayed up late last night, carefully ironing their jeans so they would look good for their first day. It was nice not to have to wear uniforms for a change.

Cristina shook her blond hair back from her face and tilted her chin. She closed her locker, but the door didn't fit right. So she slammed it. She wished Bete were with her now, but the seniors' lockers were all at the far end of the school. Cristina wondered how long it would take people to learn to call her sister "Bechee" instead of "Betty." She sighed and arranged her face in what she hoped was a confident smile, then she stepped into the flow of students.

"Cristina!" At the squeal of her name, Cristina turned and was smothered in Lisa Connors's welcome. "I just knew it was you! I've been dying for you to get here. I'm so sorry I was gone for the weekend. I couldn't help it. My parents made me go to this stupid family reunion. It was so bo-oring!"

Cristina blinked twice. Lisa had been her best friend in fourth grade—the last time the Larsons had spent a year in the States. Their families had been friends since before the girls were born. Lisa wrote occasionally, and their parents exchanged Christmas cards. Their annual photographs showed how much the girls had grown. Lisa's letters sometimes made Cristina feel like she was a trophy that Lisa pulled out when it suited her. "I have a good friend who lives in Brazil," she could boast if someone's grandmother made a trip to Europe or something.

Lisa's gush of words came to a pause, and Cristina realized she was supposed to respond. "That's okay. I was busy unpacking and getting settled," she offered.

"Oh, never mind. You're here. I can't wait to introduce you to everyone. You remember Ann."

Lisa turned to a tall girl at her side with meticulously applied makeup. Her long, softly curling hair, a shade darker than Lisa's gold, was brushed in a style that looked odd to Cristina, but she wore it with a kind of confidence that said it must be "in."

"Oh, yes, I remember Ann," Cristina replied. *How could I forget?* The month before they returned to Brazil, Lisa went off with Ann and told her all of Cristina's secrets. "You aren't going to be here anymore; I have to have other friends," Lisa had explained, as though it were the most natural thing in the world.

Ann's lips pulled back to show her upper teeth. Cristina thought it was supposed to be a smile.

"Is that the kind of earrings they're wearing in Brazil these days?" Ann asked. Cristina had studied the Connors's last Christmas picture and made sure she wore a pair of large clunky earrings like Lisa had worn. Now she noticed that both Lisa and Ann wore long, dangling earrings that swayed gently when they turned their heads.

"Why, yes," she replied. She hoped her face wasn't giving her away by turning red.

"Oh, how cute!" Lisa crooned. "I used to have some almost like those."

"Come on, Lisa. We have to get to English." Ann sounded impatient.

"What do you have now, Cris?"

Cristina consulted the schedule she had been given in the office. "Uh . . . I have English, too."

"That's great!" Lisa squeezed Cristina's arm and pulled her toward the English room. Ann joined them, her face unreadable behind her makeup.

❄ ❄ ❄

"Hi, everyone," Lisa announced to their table at lunch. "This is my friend Cris from Brazil." Cristina smiled around the long table and hoped she looked friendly rather than inane.

"Brazil? My uncle lives in Brazil. It's in Indiana," a boy explained to the broad-shouldered blond next to him. The blond wore a letterman's jacket that glittered with pins and awards. He looked like a jock straight out of one of the old-fashioned American movies they showed on Brazilian TV.

Lisa rolled her eyes. "It's in South America."

"Yeah, stupid, South America." The letterman winked at Cristina. He was good looking, and she couldn't help blushing. "You know, jungles and naked Indians and stuff." He nudged his friend and raised his eyebrows, then looked at Cristina. "Do you live in a grass hut?"

Cristina felt her face flush. He may have been cute, but he was ignorant. "Sure! And Minnesota is so cold, you live in an igloo." Cristina regretted the words as soon as they were out. She couldn't believe she would say something like that to a total stranger.

The blond hooted. The other boy elbowed him and the two of them nearly fell off the bench.

"Don't be silly, Rob!" Lisa's laugh was high-pitched and nervous. "Grass hut! How funny." She turned to Cristina. "Rob's on the football team. I bet he's quarterback next year."

Cristina suspected that Lisa's remark was a hint that Rob was popular rather than an explanation of his stupidity. Quarterback. Humph. It sounded more than ever like a bad movie. She wished she had kept her mouth shut.

"So what kind of house did you live in?" Ann asked.

"An ordinary house with a tile roof and verandas." It suddenly occurred to Cristina that the Larsons' stucco home with bougainvillea and banana trees in the garden wasn't anything like the one- and two-story boxes that passed for houses in Rum River.

"The beaches in Rio must be dreamy." Lisa seemed to have as romantic an idea of Brazil as Márcia had of the States.

"They're nice," Cristina admitted. She looked at her tray uncomfortably. Rio was as far from her home in Campo Grande as Miami was from Minnesota.

"So . . . do you live in Rio?" Ann studied her from under half-closed lids.

"No. We live in Mato Grosso do Sul—the west. It's cattle and soybean country."

"What did I tell you?" said Rob. "Cowboys and Indians." He grinned impishly and threw a wadded-up napkin the length of the table.

Cristina bit back a hot retort and tossed her head proudly. "Mato Grosso do Sul has some of the richest farms in Brazil."

"Are you rich?" someone asked.

Her pride stumbled. "No."

"Do you live on a farm?"

It felt like an interrogation with everyone staring at her. Rob's steady gaze made her hot and flustered. "No. We live in Campo Grande, the state capital."

"Why do you live there?" Ann's tone clearly implied *Why on earth would anyone want to live there?*

"My dad teaches in a seminary." Cristina knew better than to say they were missionaries.

"A what?"

This was getting touchy. "A school to train pastors," Cristina said.

"Oh. Are you a missionary or something?" From the way Ann's lip curled she might have asked if Cristina's father was an escaped convict.

Cristina wanted to lie. "Diplomats" would sound more sophisticated. "Peace Corps" would make everyone think Brazil was a temporary blip in a normal American existence.

Instead she nodded. "Um hum." Knowing looks went around the table. Missionary. Cristina could see their minds working. Definitely not rich. Probably a fanatic.

Lisa broke the silence. "It must be so exciting to get to travel."

"Actually, I'd rather stay home." Cristina looked at her tray and twisted her napkin.

"You don't like it there?" Lisa asked.

Cristina was shocked. "I meant I'd rather stay in Brazil."

❄ ❄ ❄

In fifth hour algebra class Cristina saw him. He was sitting across the aisle and one seat ahead. She tried not to stare, but he reminded her of Vicente. His hair was black and thick, and his skin looked like it could drink in the sun until it glistened like bronze.

In Brazil, Cristina's gleaming yellow hair stood out. It made her interesting, different, and attractive. Here in Minnesota, where nearly everyone was descended from Germans or Scandinavians, she looked like all the rest. This boy stood out like a raven among the cookie-cutter blondes. For the first time in her life she wished she were dark so that her outside would say to him, "I'm like you."

He was working on a chemistry assignment while the math teacher droned on in an irritating nasal voice. When she leaned forward, pretending to see the board better, she could just make out the name at the top of his paper. Jason Erickson. The name was Minnesota even if the face wasn't. Jason. She doodled a *J* in the corner of her paper and wondered what he was like.

The skinny boy in the seat ahead of her kicked Jason's foot and whispered something. Jason grinned. A short scar in his left eyebrow crinkled when he smiled and gave him a jaunty, adventurous look. He glanced at the front of the room and then back at his chemistry book.

Cristina added a fancy curl to the *J* on her paper. As she studied her handiwork, the dismissal bell rang.

"Do the exercises on pages six and seven as review," the teacher called as a babble of conversation erupted.

Cristina closed her algebra book and took her time arranging her papers.

The boy ahead of her tossed a long, blond lock from over one eye and turned to Jason. "Hey, man, you wanna shoot some hoops after school?"

"Derek," Jason's brow wrinkled. "I've got football practice."

"Oh, yeah. I forgot—drumming heads when you could be making beautiful music in the pep band."

"Oh? They're making beautiful music now?" Jason raised his eyebrows. "I didn't know you dropped out of band."

"No way!" Derek tossed his lock of hair and drummed two pencils in a wild rhythm that bounced from the desktop to his algebra book to the heel of his shoe. Cristina stared in amazement. "Ta dah!" Derek ended with a flourish.

Jason shook his head. "Like I said—what beautiful music?" He glanced at Cristina and grinned as if in conspiracy with her. The scar in his left eyebrow crinkled, and Cristina grinned back.

Jason propped his books on his hip. "Derek, my man, sometimes drumming heads is the best part of football."

❄ ❄ ❄

When classes ended, it took Cristina a full five minutes to get through the crush in the hall to her locker. Her school in Brazil, Colégio Batista, had nowhere near the eleven hundred students of crowded Rum River. Here, she felt trapped by the walled hallways, which smelled of fresh paint and cleaning fluids. She missed the open-air passages of her Brazilian school. At this time of year, the courtyard would be pungent with the scent of the orange trees in bloom.

She hung back until the girl who had snapped at her that morning slammed her locker and left. Cristina glanced at the slip of paper with her combination on it and attacked the lock. 17-08-23. Nothing happened. She twirled the dial and tried again. Nothing. She gave the locker a sharp rap with her fist. Dumb school. She'd never had a locker in Brazil.

"Hi, beautiful." Someone leaned against the locker next to her. His blond hair brushed his forehead just above vivid green eyes that sparkled like the award pins on his letterman jacket—Rob.

"Oh, hi." Cristina licked her lips. Even Minnesota didn't seem cold enough yet for Rob to need that heavy jacket. What a show-off. "Listen. I'm sorry I got so upset at lunch. I . . ." She wasn't really sorry, but it wouldn't hurt to be polite.

Rob raised his eyebrows. "I was worried," he said. "I

thought I might find piranhas in my bathtub or snakes in my bed." Cristina gave a nervous laugh. She didn't find the comment particularly funny, but she thought that was what Lisa would do. She wished he wouldn't look at her as though he were taking her measurements.

"Need help?" He took the paper from her fingers, without asking, and worked the combination. The locker opened easily.

Cristina felt like an incompetent klutz. "Thanks," she said. Burying her blushing face in the depths of the locker, she collected the things she needed for her assignments.

"You know, you have to be careful who you give your combination to," Rob said. "Someone might steal your lunch or hide a dead fish in it."

"Gross." Cristina looked sideways at him. He winked.

The halls were emptying. Over Rob's shoulder she could see Jason Erickson approaching. His T-shirt had a picture of a giant mosquito labeled "Minnesota State Bird."

"Hey, Erickson! Going to football?" Rob stuck out his foot. Jason tripped and lost his grip on his books. *Algebra Concepts* slid to the floor while he batted a thick paperback into the air. Rob winked at Cristina again. "If you're that clumsy, you'll never make the team."

"Don't you wish!" Jason replied as he snagged *A Separate Peace* on the tips of his fingers and pulled it into his chest for the catch.

Cristina picked up the math book from where it had slid against the lockers and handed it to him.

"Thanks." He added it to his pile and then looked back at Cristina. "Aren't you in my algebra class?" Cristina had a funny warm feeling inside. She smiled and nodded.

"Bug off, Erickson." Cristina frowned at Rob's possessive tone.

Jason looked from Cristina to Rob and back again. Cristina wanted to grab Jason's arm and tell him she wasn't with Rob. But she didn't.

"See you in practice, Sundquist!" Jason headed for the exit.

"Idiot—thinks he could be quarterback." Rob laughed off the idea. "No way. That's going to be me. My dad was the best quarterback this school ever had—until I get the job." Cristina wondered if he was really as confident as he sounded.

"Gotta go," Rob said. "I wouldn't want Coach to think some mongrel could play football as good as me. See ya."

He took off down the hall at a jog "Wait up, Erickson!"

Jason didn't wait.

Chapter 2

The school bus was filling up fast by the time Cristina got there. After six years she had forgotten how crowded and noisy the bus got. The one time they had come for the summer, they didn't need a school bus. Bete was already sitting with another girl.

She gestured for Cristina to join them. "Cristina, do you remember Rita?" Cristina wasn't sure she did.

Rita squeezed into the corner to make more room. "There'll be three to a seat by the time we're done, so you may as well sit with us now."

Cristina perched on the edge with her knees sticking into the aisle. She wished Rita would go away. She wanted her sister to herself. She had only glimpsed Bete once from a distance during the day, and Bete had looked as lost and confused as Cristina felt. The noise on the bus was overwhelming, and Cristina sat in dazed silence.

Rita got off with a redheaded boy whom Cristina remembered from fourth grade. He had called her "Amazon woman," and she had kicked his shin.

"How was your day?" Bete asked.

Cristina groaned. "I felt so stupid. One boy thought Brazil was in Indiana. Why do we have to be here? I just want to go home."

"I know," Bete reassured her. "In one of my classes the teacher wanted to know if I spoke Spanish. Can you imagine? The teacher didn't know that Brazilians speak Portuguese!"

They got off the bus on Kildare Road where a gravel lane led to a row of summer cottages along a lake. A list of cottage owners was posted on a sign at the corner, but they were mostly empty at this time of year. Only a retired couple named Bjork and the Larsons would stay through the winter.

Cristina glimpsed the lake to their right between the trees and cottages. It sparkled in the sunshine, but she had no desire for a swim. The first week of September was as cold as Brazilian winter. The woods to their left already showed an occasional flame of autumn red.

"We're home!" Bete yelled with her usual enthusiasm as the two girls came through the door. Cristina couldn't bring herself to call it "home," and yet there was something comfortable and familiar about the house. They had lived here every home assignment since she was a baby.

"Out here!" Mom's voice came from the deck overlooking the lake. "Bring a cup if you want coffee."

Bete hurried to the cupboard, but Cristina hesitated. She spied the iron cricket that held the front door against the breeze. Laying her book bag on the coffee table, Cristina picked up the cricket. The molded iron was cool to the touch. Her grandmother had once showed her how to place one foot on its back and wedge her other heel snuggly between its antenae. When she pulled, the boot stayed with the cricket and her foot slid neatly out.

When she was five, the iron cricket made a wonderful dragon to carry off the fairy princess. When she was in fourth grade, it was the leader of all her stuffed animal soldiers. It was hard and strong and very fierce. She told it all her secrets when Lisa stopped being her friend. There was something solid and unchanging about the cricket.

The door started to swing. Cristina grabbed it before it had a chance to slam, and wedged the cricket back in place. For now, it was enough to know it was there.

She sat down at the piano and ran through a series of scales and arpeggios. Her fingers pounded the keys as she concentrated. Strength and control. That was what *Dona* Magali insisted on. Strength and control. Cristina wanted to impress her new American teacher with all she had learned in Brazil.

The smell of strong Brazilian coffee wafted through the door from the deck. It was good to fill her mind with the music and leave no room for homesickness or worry about school. She had opened her book of Chopin etudes and started the first one when the phone rang.

"Cristina, it's for you!" Bete called from the kitchen.

"Alô." She realized what she had said as soon as it was out. She hoped the person on the other end of the line thought she had said, "hello."

"Hi, Cris. I looked all over for you after school. You don't have to ride the bus home, do you? They're just awful. Nobody rides them anymore. I've been driving to school ever since I got my license. Won't your parents let you drive?" Lisa hadn't identified herself. She didn't have to.

"I'm not sixteen yet," Cristina mumbled. No need to point out that she wouldn't even be fifteen until November. By going back and forth from Northern Hemisphere to Southern Hemisphere she had gotten ahead a year in school. Her grades were good, and it hadn't mattered when they were in fourth grade. But now, Cristina was probably the youngest junior in the history of Rum River High School.

"That's right! I forgot you're so young!" Lisa laughed. Cristina was glad Lisa couldn't see her turning red. "What about Elizabeth?"

"Well . . . there's only one car. Mom and Dad . . ."

"Oh."

Lisa didn't need to know that Bete didn't have a license either. The driving age in Brazil was eighteen. She and Bete walked or took the city bus just like everyone else in Campo Grande. But there weren't any city buses in a town as small as Rum River. And no one in America walked anywhere if they could help it.

"I just got this great new Lee Loring CD," Lisa gushed. "You've just got to hear it. Who's your favorite singer?"

Cristina thought quickly She was pretty sure that Carlos Rodriguez was not the right answer. "Lee Loring's okay."

"I think he's incredible!" Lisa crooned. "Listen to this." Cristina made a mental note that Lee Loring was a he and not a she. That *People* magazine she'd seen in the supermarket looked like an American version of *Caras*. Maybe she should read it. She didn't want to make stupid mistakes.

Lisa must have started her CD because Cristina could hear the muffled sound of music through the phone. She thought she might even have heard this song before on the radio in Brazil. Brazilian radio always played a lot of English music, even though almost no one understood the words.

Lisa chattered on. "I think Derek Patterson is so cute. Don't you just love his haircut?"

Cristina almost asked if he were a singer, too.

"Derek plays percussion in the band." Lisa rushed on, and Cristina remembered just in time that Derek was the name of Jason's friend. "What do you play? Are you going to join the band? Ann and I play in pep band. You've got to join. It's so-o much fun. What did you say you play?"

Cristina hesitated. "Uh . . . I play piano."

"Oh." There was silence for a moment at the other end of the line. "Don't you play anything else? I mean, like flute or trumpet or something?"

"No."

"That's too bad." Lisa sounded sincerely sorry. "You can come to the games anyway. If you sit across the aisle from the band, we can talk to you when we have our break. I couldn't believe the way Rob Sundquist was flirting with you at lunch. He is so cool. I mean, he's one of the best players on the football team. He got I-don't-know-how-many touchdowns last year."

Flirting? Cristina thought. *I thought we were fighting.*

Lisa babbled on. "Rob's dad was quarterback when Rum River won the state championships. The trophy's in the front hall at school. You should see it. We almost won regionals last year. It would be so-o cool if we won state again."

Cristina didn't care much about American football, but winning was always fun.

"Did you see that black guy at school?" Lisa went on. "Too bad he doesn't play football. Blacks are always good at sports. His family just moved here from St. Paul. There have never been any black people in Rum River before." She lowered her voice. "He's been hanging out with Mike McCloud, and everybody knows he's on something. You can see it in his eyes. I'll bet they both do drugs."

Cristina was shocked at the way Lisa stuffed people in boxes with little labels on them. Maybe she ought to say something, but she didn't know what. She didn't even know these kids. For all she knew Lisa might be right about them.

"Mike McCloud is an Indian and lives at the boys' farm, so what can you expect?"

"What?"

"You know, where they send the juvenile delinquents from the Cities," Lisa explained. The "Cities" with a capital

C meant Minneapolis and St. Paul. Cristina remembered that much.

"Rum River is supposed to be a 'wholesome environment' for them," Lisa said. "Instead, they poison it for the rest of us. They've started gangs and everything."

Cristina had an uncomfortable feeling that Rum River wasn't the same small town she remembered from fourth grade.

"At least the Asian kids don't cause trouble. I think Jason Erickson is really cute, and his little brother Matt is so sweet."

Cristina was puzzled. "Jason Erickson is Asian?"

"Of course he is, silly! Can't you tell by looking at him? His grandmother was Korean."

Cristina felt stupid for the two-hundred-and-forty-seventh time that day. It seemed so obvious to Lisa, but to Cristina, Jason just looked a bit closer to normal than everybody else. *I suppose Jason reminds me of the Indian blood in Brazilians,* she thought. She did remember seeing an Indian boy in the halls, but he wasn't in any of her classes.

"Jason's mother was adopted," Lisa went on. "She's just like a china doll. Jason takes after his father—you know, really strong. He plays football in the fall, hockey in the winter, and baseball in the spring." Cristina could imagine Lisa checking off his jock qualifications on her fingers.

"Jason's fun to flirt with," Lisa said, "but I'd never date him. I mean, what if you got married or something? Then your kids would be half-breeds. I think people should only date their own kind. Don't you?"

It was a totally new idea to Cristina. Nobody in Brazil cared if your ancestors came from different places. Márcia's thick black curls came from an African ancestor somewhere way back, and Vicente's bewitching eyes came from a Guarani Indian grandmother. What did it matter? Besides, if Jason was only one quarter Korean, he was more white than Asian.

Lisa babbled on. "Mark Ho asks white girls out all the time, and they always say 'no.' There's a Filipino girl in school. He should ask her out."

Cristina had only half an ear for Lisa's chatter. She wished she were home talking on the phone with Márcia about things that really mattered. She and Márcia would choose music for the praise team at church on Sunday, or maybe they would plan her *quinze anos*.

Fifteen was the most important birthday a girl could have in Brazil. At fifteen a girl was a young lady, and her fifteenth birthday party was a gala affair full of traditions. Americans didn't care anything about *quinze anos*. They thought sweet sixteen was the important one, and even then they usually didn't do anything special.

"Did you do anything special for your birthday?" She interrupted Lisa before she gave herself time to think about it.

"My birthday?"

"Yeah. You were sixteen, weren't you? Isn't that supposed to be special?"

Lisa sounded surprised. "I suppose so. But nobody has a big party anymore. I had a few friends sleep over. We watched videos and ate pizza. Why? In Brazil do girls have a big party for their sixteenth birthday?"

"No. Fifteenth. It's when a girl becomes a young lady."

"You mean like a coming-out party for society girls?" Cristina could hear the excitement in Lisa's voice.

"I suppose so." Cristina wasn't sure what a coming-out party was. "All the girls wear white lace dresses, and there are fourteen girls and fourteen boys. The birthday girl and her father make the fifteenth couple." She sighed, remembering. "The best part of the party comes when the girl dances the waltz with her father, and then each of them takes a different partner and so on until fifteen couples are dancing!"

Lisa drew in her breath. "Like a romance novel!"

"Márcia's party was wonderful!" Cristina went on. "Márcia's my best friend." If Lisa was hurt by Cristina's enthusiasm for her Brazilian friend, Cristina was too caught up in her own thoughts to notice. "Her party was at the *Clube Royale*. We had a private dining room that opened onto the terrace. It was a wonderful summer night. Live musicians play the waltz. The cake was like a small wedding cake, and there was an elegant crystal punch bowl. And Vicente, Márcia's brother, danced with me more than anyone else."

"How old is he? Is he good-looking?"

"Seventeen and very! He's the best-looking *gato* I know.

We were practically *namorando*. You would say dating," she explained, trying to sound blasé about it. She was only exaggerating a little. He had danced with her more than once that evening, and she was sure they would be dating by now—if she hadn't been forced by her parents to come to the States.

"Are you going to have a fancy party, too?" Lisa's voice tingled with expectancy.

"Márcia and I used to plan our parties by the hour." Cristina didn't really say yes or no. She wanted to impress Lisa by saying she would. But she knew it wasn't likely to happen. Fancy parties were expensive. Her parents never spent money on stuff like that. They spent money on important things, like a new computer for the seminary or medicine for *Dona* Benedita's baby. Bete had a small reception at home. Bete had no imagination!

She sighed. "Probably not. This isn't Brazil. Where would we have it? The roller rink? No one would understand. I mean, how many of my friends know how to waltz?"

That silenced Lisa. "I've got some great CDs we could dance to," she suggested, her voice tentative.

"It's not the same." Cristina couldn't hide her frustration. "The waltz is a tradition."

Lisa sighed. "It would have been so romantic."

Chapter 3

"Is school lunch in Brazil as bad as it is here?" Lisa asked the next day. Using a carrot stick, she turned over a clump of soggy macaroni and cheese

After Ann's interrogation the first day, Cristina had promised herself she wouldn't talk about Brazil, but she couldn't ignore Lisa. "We don't eat lunch at school."

"You don't eat lunch?" Ann eyed Cristina's figure critically. "Is that why you're so skinny?"

Cristina wished she had ignored Lisa after all. How could she explain that everyone went home for lunch? That was when Brazilians ate their main meal. In the evening, the Larsons usually just warmed up some leftovers or ate crispy French bread with strong coffee and hot milk. Her father always came home from the seminary at noon and they had rice and beans with salad and meat. The thought of savory rice and beans made her mouth water. She pushed the tasteless macaroni away. "I go to school mornings."

"You don't have to go all day?"

"No. Some students go mornings and some afternoons. Of course, I have to be there at 6:45!"

"Jason! Derek!" cooed Lisa. "Come sit with us." Cristina looked up into Jason's warm brown eyes and something fluttered in her chest.

"Hi." He looked straight at her. He couldn't be talking to anyone else.

Derek tossed the dangling blond lock out of his eye and winked.

Lisa scooted closer to Cristina and made room for the two of them on her other side. "You have to meet my friend, Cris Larson. She's from Brazil. South America," she added, aiming a meaningful look up the table at the boy who had thought it was in Indiana.

He laughed and threw a spoonful of gelatin at the ceiling. It stuck.

"Yeah, I've met Cris," Jason said. He leaned forward to look around Lisa with a sly grin that crinkled the scar in his eyebrow.

Cristina felt her cheeks grow warm. She nodded.

"Jason's on the football team," Lisa interrupted. She squeezed Jason's arm and batted her eyelashes at him. "He's almost as good as Rob Sundquist. Everyone's wondering who's going to be quarterback next year when Jim Carlson graduates." She giggled and cast a flirtatious glance toward the other end of the table.

Ann looked disgusted, and for once Cristina agreed with her.

"What do you mean, 'almost as good'?" Derek demanded. "You should have seen Rob limping around after Jason kept hitting him in practice yesterday."

Jason laughed. "I got a few bruises myself." He took a bite of macaroni, and his expression turned grim. He reached for the ketchup.

"It's no good," Ann said. "Try a carrot."

"How about you, Derek?" Lisa crooned. "Didn't you go out for football this year?"

"Well," Derek admitted. "Coach hasn't noticed my talent. Actually . . . he doesn't think I weigh enough. Can you imagine that?" He spread his lanky arms in disbelief. "So I'll be back in the band this year . . ."—he placed his hand over his heart—". . . playing the school song for the honor of old Rum River High."

"Awww." Lisa gave him a look of exaggerated concern. Derek grinned impishly at Cristina as though female sympathy was what he wanted all along.

"Hey, Erickson," Rob called from the other end of the table. "Did you watch that kung fu movie last night? All those slant-eyes running around with the pretty girls."

"No, Rob." Jason pushed his uneaten macaroni and ketchup away. "I don't watch that kind of stuff. Did you enjoy it?"

Rob laughed raucously and his buddy made a few karate chops in the air.

Jason turned back to Cristina. "Coming to the game on Friday?"

"Me?" She gulped.

"Of course she's coming," insisted Lisa. "Nobody wants to miss the first football game of the season."

Cristina hadn't thought about it. She and Bete used to go to the games with their parents when they were little. "You can sleep over at my house," Lisa added as though it were all settled.

With Jason playing, it might be interesting, even though she didn't know anything about American football. "I'll come," she said.

Jason nodded his satisfaction, then dug a fork into his jello.

Ann launched into an elaborate story that included the names of people Cristina didn't know and connections she couldn't quite follow. A girl on the other side of her started talking about a baby-sitting job, and loud laughter erupted from the table behind them. Cristina was quickly confused by the cacophony of sounds.

"I think I've got a zit," said Lisa, fingering her chin.

"What's a zit?" Cristina asked, and immediately wished she had bitten her tongue instead.

"What's a zit?" Suddenly everyone's eyes were on Cristina, including the big brown ones whose attention she had craved. Now she wished they would look anywhere but at her.

"You don't know what a zit is?" Ann threw back her head and howled with laughter. "You don't have that perfect a complexion, do you?"

For one horrible moment everyone studied her face closely for telltale marks, and Cristina realized with horror that a zit must be a pimple. She hoped she had adequately covered with makeup the few she had that morning.

"I think I just figured it out," she murmured weakly. She wished she could crawl under the table or make herself small enough to drown in the ketchup bottle.

Lisa was amused. "You know those little red things that pop out on your face when you least want them?" she teased. She poked maliciously at her own flawless complexion with the fingers of both hands as though it were a mass of oozing pustules.

Ann tilted her head and curled her lip. "What do you call them?"

"Espinhas," Cristina admitted timidly.

"Pee on us?" Ann deliberately mispronounced the strange word. "Is that supposed to be Spanish?"

Cristina felt her face grow hot. "Portuguese," she snapped. Her embarrassment was fast turning to anger.

"Oh, come on! Don't tease her," Lisa patted Cristina's hand sympathetically. "How is she supposed to know?"

The idea that ignorance was to be expected wasn't very comforting. Jason's big brown eyes took a sudden interest in his jello.

"C'mon," said Lisa. "I wanna use the restroom before class." Cristina followed, not daring to look back at Jason.

❄ ❄ ❄

After school Cristina picked up the iron cricket and headed for the room she shared with her sister. Curling up on the bed, she clasped the cricket in her arms. It felt cold and hard against her. Lisa had thought it was "gross" when in fourth grade she found out that Cristina played with an insect. Cristina didn't care. The cricket didn't say silly things or think she was stupid. He didn't say anything at all. And she wasn't stupid! Just different.

It's hard to be different, she thought. She longed for her home in Brazil and familiar things and people. She knew where she fit in Brazil. Here she felt like a stranger caught between two worlds, an interesting diversion for Lisa, a disruption for Ann, but not part of the group. If Lisa weren't there, would anyone sit with her at lunch? Was there anyone she wanted to sit with? A vision of dark, inquiring brown eyes filled her mind. But she would never have the courage to sit down with him, and after today he would never look at her again.

She longed for Márcia, who had shared her secrets for years. Márcia wouldn't know what a zit was any more than she did, even though Márcia did reasonably well in English. Who cared anyway? What difference did it make? She buried her face in the pillow and sobbed, hugging the iron cricket with all her strength. She knew it did make a difference knowing what a zit was. It was the difference between being one of the girls and an outsider, between being in-the-know or ignorant, at home or a foreigner in her parents' homeland.

After a while she stopped crying. The cricket's unyielding limbs and antennae poked relentlessly into her stomach. Márcia wouldn't understand any better than Lisa.

After all, Márcia had only visited the United States as a tourist. She had never lived here. If she came to Rum River High School, she'd be a foreigner.

Two foreign exchange students attended the school—one from Norway and another from Japan. Cristina didn't know if they were homesick or not, but it didn't seem to bother them to be different. It was expected. Maybe her problem was that she was neither fish nor fowl, as her grandfather would say. She was a foreigner in Brazil because her family was American, but she was just as much a foreigner here because she felt Brazilian. *No place is really home,* she thought with despair.

Cristina had always been taught to pray about her problems, but today she didn't know what to say even to God. Make me different from who I am? That wasn't really what she wanted God to do. Make Mom and Dad decide to go home to Brazil right now? She knew very well what God would say to a prayer like that.

"At least You could help me not to act like a stupid idiot." She swung her legs over the side of the bed, got up, and went to the mirror. Running a brush through her hair so it wouldn't look so rumpled, she checked her face in the mirror. She didn't think anyone could tell she'd been crying.

She couldn't write all this to Márcia, but maybe she could write it down for herself. She pulled out the diary that Mom and Dad had given to her last Christmas. It was a blank book covered with pink flowers on a black background. Several enthusiastic entries were dated from last January and some around the time of Márcia's birthday party. But most of the pages were blank. Either there was nothing to write about or no time to write.

She wrote the date and began, "Today I made a complete fool of myself at lunch right in front of the most beautiful brown eyes in the world, next to Vicente's."

Chapter 4

"If you had a fancy birthday party, this is what I'd wear," Lisa said. She struck one fashion-model pose after another in the dressing room mirror. Dark green lace swirled around her legs.

Cristina chewed her lower lip and ran her fingers over the silky blue satin she was trying on. It accented the color of her eyes and brought a rosy glow to her cheeks. She felt very elegant and grown up in it.

The girls had spent Friday afternoon, browsing in gift shops and trying on clothes in the strip mall that had replaced some old houses just off Main Street. Cristina saw some jeans like Ann wore, the kind with the brand name sewn on the pocket. But they cost more than she had to spend. She bought a top that Lisa said was really in. It looked sophisticated, and the deep rose color suited her.

They had paraded in front of the mirrors, wearing slinky outfits they wouldn't have been caught dead in outside the fitting room. Then they had explored the evening wear. It had been a fun day—like one she might have spent with

Márcia at home. Having fun with Lisa felt vaguely uncomfortable, like being disloyal to her Brazilian friends.

She looked longingly at her reflection. Even though white lace was traditional, it wouldn't be appropriate in this climate—not in November. Cristina glanced at the price tag, while pretending to adjust the sleeve. Chewing the corner of her lip, she did the arithmetic to figure out the cost in Brazilian *reais*. She gulped. There wouldn't be a *quinze anos* anyway, so what was the point in thinking about it? She jerked on the zipper and stepped out of the dress.

"Come on," she said. "We have to hurry if we're going to have time for a sandwich before the game."

❋ ❋ ❋

The outside door to the band room was open when she and Lisa arrived. It had rained in the afternoon and the air smelled clean and fresh. The rain had stopped and bits of pale blue twilight showed through the clouds.

Cristina stood shyly just inside the door while Lisa got her clarinet and others pushed by with their instruments. A pleasant babble of confusion rose around her.

"What are you doing here?" Ann demanded.

"I came with Lisa. I'm just waiting until it's time to go over to the game," Cristina defended herself.

"You know you can't go in with the band. Only those with instruments get in free."

"I know. You don't have to tell me." Cristina's voice had

an edge she hadn't intended. Ann could be so unpleasant when Lisa wasn't around and Cristina usually found herself being equally unpleasant back.

The students found seats and warmed up their instruments. Phrases of the school song and of various themes crossed each other and fought for attention. An electric charge of anticipation filled the air.

Cristina wished she were a part of it. If only she played a band instrument, but Brazilian schools didn't have music programs. Even the Campo Grande Civic Orchestra sounded only about like Rum River's Middle School band the first day of practice.

"All right, let's get started." Mr. Richards tapped the music stand with his baton. "A quick run-through of the fight song." He raised his baton and the instruments came up as one. The music began with his downward stroke.

Three measures into it Mr. Richards stopped. "Where's Steve?"

Everyone turned to stare toward the percussion section.

"He jammed his finger in PE today," Derek explained. "They think it's broken. He'll probably be out for a while."

Mr. Richards looked lost for a moment. "We can't play the school fight song without a bass drum." He ran his fingers through his hair as he surveyed the band.

"Cris could play it," Lisa piped up from the front row.

All eyes turned her way, and Cristina felt the color rising to her cheeks. What did she know about playing the bass drum? She had never hit one in her life. But if she could play it, she'd be in the band! Maybe more than just tonight. How long did it take a broken finger to heal?

"Cris is great on the piano," Lisa explained to Mr. Richards. "She can read music and keep the rhythm."

Mr. Richards looked at her thoughtfully.

"I can try," Cristina offered, not daring to believe he would say yes.

"Go ahead. Derek, give her the music and show her how to hit it."

Cristina could hardly believe her luck. She stepped quickly behind the rest of the band, past Derek with his snare drums, to where the bass drum waited. She was desperately afraid that Mr. Richards would change his mind.

Derek tossed back his long lock of hair and showed her the music. It was simple!—nothing more than little Xs with stems and measure lines. It looked like beginning piano exercises for small children who were learning to count rhythms without worrying about notes.

"Hit it with a flick of your wrist," Derek explained. "Don't just thunk it." He demonstrated the difference in the sound and handed her the heavy padded stick. Her hands were sweaty when she took it from him, and she paused to wipe them on her jeans. She hit the drum a couple of times, listened with satisfaction to the resonating sound, and then nodded to Mr. Richards that she was ready.

"From the top," he said.

This time when the baton came down, Cristina was playing right along with all the other members of the band. She remembered the melody from fourth grade. She used to jump up and down and clap her hands with the bass drum. Now she was playing it.

When they finished the song, Mr. Richards gave her a smile and a nod. "Try the national anthem. Cris, play whatever you feel comfortable with. You're doin' great!"

They played bits of several other pieces, and Christina's self-confidence increased as she easily followed the music. She fervently hoped that Steve's finger would take a very long time to heal.

"You were great!" Lisa exclaimed to Christina when they broke up to walk down to the field. "You're in the band! I knew you could do it."

Derek showed her how to put the drum's straps over her shoulders and fasten the waist strap to hold the weight. It was awkward, but Cristina wasn't about to complain. Derek was friendlier than he had ever been before. She didn't feel like Lisa's tagalong anymore.

When the band passed the stands to reach their position, Cristina spotted Bete and Rita where they sat together. She waved her drumstick madly and grinned when Bete's mouth fell open. The smell of apple cider and popcorn drifted up from the refreshment booth under the stands, and Cristina was reminded of all the football games she had ever been to in this town. Suddenly, being in America didn't seem so bad.

The band launched into a jazz tune so lively that if Cristina hadn't been beating the drum, she would have had to get up and dance with the cheerleaders. The trumpets had their part; the flutes had theirs; so did the saxophones and the French horns. Each one was different, but together it was music, and over it all were the drums, keeping the rhythm going at a pace that wouldn't let you sit still.

Shortly before kickoff, the band played "The Star Spangled Banner." It was a good thing Cristina was in the band. She hadn't sung it in so long she couldn't remember what came after "dawn's early light." A cheer went up even before the anthem ended. Cristina was so startled she almost missed the beat. It seemed disrespectful to treat the national anthem like a team fight song. You might as well start yelling after the hymn in church.

Rum River kicked the ball to the visiting team. Cristina had a moment to check the program. Jason's number was twenty-four. She finally found it among the jerseys that were crashing into the visitors. The program listed Rob Sundquist as number nineteen under "offensive."

Figures, Cristina thought. *He's offensive enough.*

Cristina watched the back of Jason's white jersey as the line moved forward across the field. He dodged several players and headed straight for the runner with the ball. His timing was flawless. Another Rum River player forced the visitor Jason's way. Jason crashed into him and pulled him to the ground.

"Ouch." Cristina cringed. Even with all that padding, it had to hurt.

"Way to go, Jason!" Derek yelled at her side.

The trumpets stood along the top row of the stands and played a short melody that ended on a high note. The entire Rum River side stood on cue and shouted "Charge!"

"Charge!" Cristina yelled a half second after everyone else and hit the drum a few times to add to the cheering.

Both players, streaked with mud from the damp field, got to their feet. Everyone lined up again. When the teams went into their little groups for the third time in five minutes, Cristina wanted to ask Derek why they kept stopping. But she kept her mouth shut for once. She thought she remembered something about having three or four chances to go a certain distance.

The players lined up and piled on top of each other again. This time when they got up everyone ran off the field and a whole new team came from the benches.

This is so confusing, Cristina thought. *Not anything like real* futebol. *I mean, soccer.*

Cristina didn't find the game as interesting when number twenty-four wasn't out there, but it was fun just to be a part of the band. She wasn't on the outside of Rum River High School anymore. She was on the inside—part of a group.

It wasn't that she didn't make mistakes. She did. And bass drum mistakes tended to be loud and embarrassing. Sometimes she forgot to flick her wrist and the sound came out like a dull thunk, but no one seemed to mind. They hardly even noticed amid the fun and excitement of being at the game.

"Hey, Jason!" yelled a boy of eleven or twelve along the chain link fence. Jason turned around on the bench and waved.

That has to be Matt, Cristina thought. He had Jason's face, even if he didn't yet have Jason's height or muscular shoulders.

A petite woman beside him hooked her thumbs in the pockets of her jeans. When the crowd yelled she craned her neck to see over the players' bench onto the field. Her dark hair curved gracefully around a delicate chin, and Cristina guessed that this was Jason's mom.

The team came out of the huddle and lined up. Cristina saw Rob's number nineteen behind the quarterback. Sometimes Jim Carlson gave the ball to him and sometimes he passed it to someone else. This time he thrust the ball at a Rum River player, who ran fast toward the bleachers with his arms clutched to his chest. The people in front of her stood up, and Cristina had to stand to see over them.

"Awww!" Derek moaned. "We'll never get the first down." The players on the field had stopped running, and a pile at the far side untangled itself. Rob got up from the bottom with the ball.

"How did he get the ball?" Cristina asked.

"It was a fake," Derek explained. "One of our best plays."

A man at the fence yelled and shook his right fist at the referees—his left sleeve dangled empty. The back of his neck flamed with anger.

"That's Mr. Sundquist, Rob's dad," Derek explained. "Lost his arm in Vietnam. He thinks there should have been a flag on the play."

Cristina wasn't sure what a flag meant, but some of the crowd seemed to agree with Rob's dad. The ref didn't.

Rob started toward the referee on the field, but another Rum River player pulled him back. Rob shook him off and headed for the bench with the rest of the team following. He jerked off his helmet and punched it with his fist, looking as angry as his father.

✳ ✳ ✳

After the halftime show, the band had a break.

"Come on. Let's get something to drink." Lisa pushed against the crowd to come three rows back and pull Cristina after her down the bleacher steps.

Ann bought popcorn and shared it around. It made Cristina thirsty. Fizz tickled her nose as she gulped her cola from the paper cup on their way back to the bleachers.

Mr. Sundquist was yelling and shaking his fist as the girls passed him. "Get that slant-eyed idiot off the field and put in someone who can play football!"

Cristina cringed. No wonder Rob talked the way he did. She wondered if he were embarrassed for his dad to act that way in public.

"You shut up about my brother!" Matt Erickson lunged toward the man.

"Matt!" His mother gripped his shirt.

Mr. Sundquist ignored him. At that moment the crowd rose behind them, and every eye was on the field. The visiting quarterback had his arm drawn back to throw, but he hesitated. Jason broke through the line and headed straight for the quarterback. The visitor took a few steps backward and dodged left to avoid Jason. But Jason kept coming. The quarterback ran backward several more steps.

"Sack him, Jason!" Matt screamed.

Jason reached the red jersey and brought it down almost at the Rum River goal line. Cristina and Lisa jumped up and down and hugged each other.

"Yes!" Matt yelled, practically climbing the fence in his eagerness.

It was a good thing Cristina had nearly finished her drink. The ice was all over the ground.

Mr. Sundquist glowered.

❄ ❄ ❄

In the fourth quarter Jason removed all doubt as to who was the star of the game. The visitors had the ball where the white line said "40" on the Rum River end of the field. Cristina fiddled with her drumstick and watched Jason crouch behind the line.

The visiting quarterback took a few steps back and looked around. Two Rum River players broke through in different spots. The quarterback had to hurry. He slipped in the mud as he threw the ball. It didn't go close enough to his player. It was almost as close to Jason. Both boys ran toward where the ball would come down, but Jason was faster. He stretched a long arm and caught it easily, just as he had the book in the hall at school. He pulled it into his chest and ran, trailing visiting players like the tail of a comet.

The crowd stood and cheered. "Go, Jason!" Cristina screamed. "Run! Run!" She saw Matt Erickson along the fence, going wild with excitement. He threw his body to the left as though he could help Jason avoid a tackle. Only Mr. Sundquist stood with his hands in his pockets as though it didn't matter.

Jason dodged left, and an opponent slid in the mud behind him. He ran behind two Rum River players who forced the visitors out of the way. A Rum River player went down. Jason leaped over him and ran on. A visiting player got close enough to grab Jason's jersey. Jason twisted in a circle. It slowed him, but it didn't stop him. He broke away, ten yards to go and no one near. Jason crossed the goal line. Touchdown!

Everyone was screaming as though they had just won the state tournament. Cristina yelled as loudly as any of them. Mr. Richards raised his baton for the school song. Cristina was so busy watching the field that she missed the first two measures, but once she started, she hit the drum for all she was worth. This was for Jason.

"That was so much fun!" Cristina lugged the drum to the band room after the game.

Mr. Richards jogged ahead to unlock the door. "If Steve is still out next time, you'd be welcome to join us, Cris."

"Okay," was all Cristina said, but something inside her swelled like a trumpet fanfare.

Chapter 5

Cristina followed Lisa into the Connors's kitchen. Staying with Lisa for the weekend was a lot better than traveling to North Dakota with her parents. Mom and Dad were visiting one of the churches that sent money for the work in Brazil.

When the girls were little, they went along. It was always the same. They stood up front and sang a song in Portuguese, Dad preached, sometimes Mom gave a children's talk, Cristina and Bete played with the kids. Sometimes they had a lot of fun, but then they went away and never saw those kids again. Her life was one good-bye after another. This year Cristina said she didn't want to go. She was surprised when her parents agreed to let her stay with the Connors. Bete was staying with Rita.

The breakfast table was cluttered with milk and cereal boxes. Lisa's dad had the local paper opened to the ad page.

"Hmm," he mused. "They've got a special on snowmobile oil at Hank's Hardware."

"We'll go," Lisa offered. Cristina suspected she would jump at any excuse to drive.

"It seems a little early to get the snowmobile out," Mr. Connors said. "The leaves have barely started to turn."

"But now's when they have the sale. Today would be a great day to work on the snowmobile. Cris and I'd be happy to run into town."

Mr. Connors got a pencil and paper from beside the phone. "You're right. It won't get any warmer for working in the garage. I'll make a list."

The list was done by the time the girls had finished breakfast.

"I don't know how you stand riding the bus," Lisa said as she slid behind the driver's seat. "I'd rather go to school by snowmobile." She laughed. "In fact, if they allowed it, I'll bet half the school would come on snowmobiles in winter." She flicked on the radio to a popular station, and a lively beat filled the car. Cristina checked the dial so she would know which station to listen to at home.

"Let's go the back way." Lisa turned right as she exited the drive instead of left to the highway. They wound between lakes and farm ponds toward the community college building on the hill.

"Do lots of kids have snowmobiles?" Cristina asked. She had a vivid memory of holding on for dear life behind Lisa's dad at a family outing six years ago. She was absolutely terrified—and longed to go again.

Lisa looked at her as if she had asked something as dumb as "What's a zit?" "Everybody has snowmobiles. Don't you?"

"It's not really practical when we aren't here that much." Cristina knew she sounded exactly like her mother.

"Dad's a fanatic. Last year he gave himself a Christmas present of a sled to carry ice fishing equipment. He went on and on about how useful it would be in an emergency. Yeah, right. I think he's just a big boy who likes expensive toys."

Cristina laughed. Her dad had a weakness for camping equipment.

The song ended and the news began. "In Washington a Connecticut congressman has resigned over allegations . . ." Lisa turned down the volume. "I like snowmobiling, too. There's a great trail around Hubbard Lake."

"A plane is down in the Pantanal region of Brazil, South America." Cristina caught the announcer's words through Lisa's chatter. He had mispronounced Pantanal, but he definitely said "Brazil." She reached for the volume control.

"Sh! sh!" She gestured frantically for Lisa to be quiet.

"Four Americans are among those missing and feared dead."

"What's the matter?" Lisa asked, making it impossible for Cristina to hear.

"In sports, spokespersons for the NBA Players Union say . . ."

"Is that all?" Cristina demanded of the radio. "Aren't they going to tell us how many others were on the plane? The Americans weren't the only ones unless it was a private charter." She hit the dash in frustration. "The Pantanal is as big as the state of New York. Can't they tell us where in the Pantanal? Are there any survivors?" The radio babbled on about strike negotiations and how much money was being lost by overpaid athletes and owners.

"Good grief, Cris, what difference does it make? You can't do anything anyway," Lisa said.

Cristina stared at her. "What difference does it make?" She fumbled for words. "If it were a plane crash in Minnesota, wouldn't you want to know what happened? What if someone you knew were on that plane? Márcia's dad flies to Cuiabá all the time."

"Where's that?"

Cristina waved her hand in disgust. She felt sick. Lisa was right. There was nothing she could do about it. Maybe there would be more on the TV news this evening. She doubted it. American news was all about America. Nobody seemed to care what went on in the rest of the world. Brazilians paid attention to what went on in America. America was so big they had to. But here they wouldn't even have mentioned the crash if there hadn't been Americans on board. It was like no one else mattered. She stared glumly at the dash, but she wouldn't say anything more. Lisa had accused her once of whining.

Lisa steered around a corner. "Look, Cris, I'm sorry about your friend. Maybe you can call or something."

"Yeah. Dad will call the Almeidas if he thinks there's something to be concerned about." She sighed. She wished she could stop the car and call right now.

"That's Jason Erickson's house up ahead." Lisa pointed to a neat split-level with an attached garage. Cristina tried not to show too much interest. "There's his mom's car," Lisa said.

A blue Honda backed out of the driveway while the garage door descended automatically. As Cristina turned her head to watch, the Honda stopped with a jerk.

"Wait!" said Cristina. Lisa slowed down and looked at her. "Go back," Cristina insisted. "Something's wrong."

"You like Jason, don't you?" Lisa teased as she stopped the car and backed up. "Oh, my Lord!" It was the strongest language Lisa's parents would let her use.

The garage door was a mess. Cristina stared at the hateful words spray painted across the green aluminum. They made it clear that foreigners were not wanted in Rum River. Mrs. Erickson's head was bent forward over the steering wheel as though she didn't want to look.

Lisa turned off the car and got out. Cristina followed. "Mrs. Erickson, are you all right?" Lisa tapped on the car window. Mrs. Erickson's head jerked up. Her face was pale and frightened.

Mrs. Erickson nodded and put her hand to her lips. She opened the window and her voice quivered, "Yes, yes. I'm all right. It just startled me so." She opened the door and got out. "I can't imagine who would do a thing like this. Thank goodness the boys are at their father's this weekend." She patted her jacket pockets nervously. "I have to get it cleaned up before they see it. Jason would be so angry."

"We can help," said Cristina. "Some dark green paint should cover it. Shouldn't you tell the police first?"

"Yes . . . yes. I suppose they have to know. But I don't want the boys to know. Matt is too young to understand. There's extra paint in the garage. Jim was always planning to redo the trim, but he never got to it. And I . . ." She looked very vulnerable. "It's so . . . ugly."

It was ugly. Cristina and Lisa went home and changed into painting clothes and brought Mr. Connors back with a ladder. By that time Mrs. Erickson had calmed down, and the police were just leaving.

"We'll let you know if we find out anything," one said as they climbed into the cruiser.

"Just some kid's prank, I'm sure," Mrs. Erickson said. "Doesn't mean anything. I'd just rather the boys not know about it. Jason is awfully protective since his father left."

"I can understand that," said Mr. Connors. He pulled a couple of paint tarps out of the back of his pickup. Lisa helped him.

"You don't have to do this," Mrs. Erickson insisted. "I can manage. I'm sure you had other plans."

"Nothing that can't wait," Mr. Connors replied. Cristina couldn't imagine leaving her alone.

Cristina spread green paint across the black words. Somehow helping Mrs. Erickson made her feel better about not being able to help anyone in Brazil. "It's a good thing the door isn't white," she commented. "One coat wouldn't be enough."

"Who on earth would do something like this?" Lisa wondered aloud.

Cristina was afraid she knew.

❋ ❋ ❋

A clump of band members milled around Cristina's locker on Monday morning. It was fun to be part of a crowd.

"And here comes the man of the hour!" announced Derek. He drummed a fanfare with two pencils on her locker as Jason came down the hall.

"Hi, Jason."

"Jason! Great game!" Every girl in the school seemed to want to congratulate him.

"Good job, Erickson!" A boy with double ear piercings gave him a high five. Jason's grin kept bursting through any attempts to be modest.

"Jason, it was so-o cool." Lisa tucked her arm through his. "I couldn't believe how you dodged all those other players and just kept going and going like that bunny on TV. It was so-o exciting."

Jason laughed, then he grinned at Cristina. "I hear that was you on the bass."

Cristina felt her cheeks go red. "Yeah."

"Y' done good." He grinned at his mockery of grammar and raised his hand in a high five.

Cristina's stomach quivered with butterflies as she hit it.

She dug her grammar book out from under three novels and two issues of *People* in her locker.

"Erickson." Cristina jerked up her head at the sound of Rob's voice. "Have a nice weekend?" His voice was as smooth as if Jason were his best friend.

Jason looked surprised. "It was okay." Cristina was sure he didn't know what had happened.

"I see you painted your garage."

Lisa stopped in the middle of what she was saying to Ann. Cristina held her breath, as tense as Jason waiting for the snap.

"Yeah. What's it to you?" Jason answered.

Rob smirked at him, then winked at Cristina. "Nothing," he said.

Cristina stared at Rob's jeans. A faint dusting of black had left a stain, like from a can of spray paint. Rob looked down and brushed nervously at it. It didn't come off. He closed his locker and joined his friends. Cristina let out her breath very slowly.

"You guys going to class," Jason asked, "or are you hanging around here all day?" Cristina could hardly believe it when he waited for her to close her locker.

"You painted the garage?" Derek asked as they started down the hall.

"My mom did it. Matt and I were at Dad's for the weekend. I couldn't believe it. We got home Sunday afternoon, and she had the door and trim done. Next weekend she wants Matt and me to put up security lights. Suddenly we're into 'home improvement.'"

"Your mother painted the garage?" Derek repeated it as though he still couldn't believe it. Cristina didn't dare to look at Lisa.

"Yeah. I don't know why she picked this weekend. The stuff has been in the garage since. . . ," he hesitated, and Cristina remembered his mother saying her husband had bought it before he left. " . . . for ages," Jason finished.

"Hey! Wasn't Cris great in the band?" Lisa interrupted. She patted Cristina proudly on the shoulder. "Who do we play this weekend?"

"Apple Valley." Derek raised a clenched fist. "We're gonna cream 'em! We're on a roll!"

Cristina had a feeling Rob would not agree.

Chapter 6

Cristina hoped this wasn't a mistake. Lisa wanted to do the mall again before the game—this time with Ann. It wasn't like Cristina could say no without admitting she was jealous. Then Mom suggested she invite Lisa to stay the night and somehow Ann got invited, too. Cristina felt trapped, but it would be rude to tell Lisa she didn't want Ann to come. Lisa wouldn't understand.

Cristina followed slowly as Lisa dragged Ann through the women's department. "You've got to see the gorgeous dress I found."

From the rack, Lisa pulled the gown she had chosen last week and held it in front of her. "Isn't it elegant?" She spun on her toes and dark green lace billowed around her.

"I like this one better," Ann said. She held up a black velvet, strapless gown with sequins down the front.

Cristina fingered the softness of the blue satin she had admired last week. She knew she couldn't buy it, but she checked the tag once again. After all, they could have marked the price down since last week. They hadn't.

"Don't I look sophisticated?" Ann struck a pose with

the black velvet held in front of her. It looked silly with her jeans sticking out beneath.

Lisa giggled. "It's too much for Cristina's birthday party."

"Birthday party?" Ann stared.

Cristina couldn't believe Lisa had told her. "Lisa! I'm not going to have a fancy party." She should have kept her secrets for the iron cricket.

"Oh, but it would be so cool!" Lisa cooed. "Can't you just see me in this dress?" She cocked her chin at a jaunty angle and pranced around.

Ann put the black velvet back on the rack. "What birthday party?" she insisted.

Cristina took a deep breath. "I'll be fifteen November fifth. That's a special birthday in Brazil." She hated mentioning Brazil around Ann. It always felt like she was showing off when she didn't mean to. Ann inevitably found a reason to put down the only life she had. "Sometimes . . . girls have a party . . ."

"They dance the waltz and everything, Ann," Lisa put in. "It would be so elegant!"

"A waltz?" Ann actually looked interested. She fingered a more modest black satin with a flared skirt.

"Ann's a wonderful dancer," Lisa told Cristina. "She's taken lessons for years. I'll bet she could teach the rest of us."

Cristina rolled her eyes in frustration. "Lisa! It isn't going to happen. Can you imagine fifteen couples dancing the waltz in our family room?"

"There's the fireside room at church," Ann suggested. "It looks really classy when they fix it up for wedding receptions. There'd be plenty of room for dancing if we moved the chairs."

"Ooh! There's a grand piano and everything," Lisa added. "And a kitchen right off it. It's perfect."

"Forget it, Lisa. I'm going to look at shoes."

❄ ❄ ❄

The subject drifted in the back of Cristina's mind for the rest of the afternoon. The fireside room had large arching windows with elegant burgundy drapes. She found herself studying a pair of black heels with delicate crisscross bands, and wondering if the heels were low enough for dancing comfortably. She saw Lisa and Ann talking excitedly, but they stopped abruptly when she came within hearing range.

They met other band members in the sandwich shop before the game. Someone teased them about being the three musketeers. Ann laughed, but Cristina was embarrassed.

The resounding boom of the bass drum greeted them as they entered the band room. Cristina looked up with her stomach in her mouth. There was a tall thin boy standing near Derek, swinging the padded stick with an accomplished flourish and letting it hit the head of the drum with a satisfying boom. A painful cramp under Cristina's ribs made her wish she had said no to jalapeño peppers on her sub.

"Steve! What are you doing back?" Lisa crossed the room with her usual flare.

Steve raised his right hand and wiggled his index finger. "It was just jammed. The doctor took the splint off this afternoon. It's still a little bruised but what the—" He gave the drum a firm whack.

"That's great," said Lisa. Cristina couldn't see her face, but she knew the eyelashes were fluttering. "Cris did a good job last week while you were out."

Steve looked toward the doors and waved. "Thanks, Cris." Cristina smiled and waved back. Her cheeks felt like Play-Doh molded into shape.

"I have to get my flute," Ann said. She brushed Cristina's arm as she passed. It almost seemed like she was sorry for Cristina.

Cristina leaned against the wall exactly where she had waited last week while the band warmed up. The themes and bits of melody clashed and broke off like the thoughts in her head. When Mr. Richards pulled them to order and the first few bars of the school song came together, it felt like there was sand in her eyes. She blinked several times to get it out. The bass drum never thunked once. Each stroke was deep and solid.

When the band walked over to the football field, Cristina trailed along, glad she still had enough pocket money to buy a ticket. That lost and empty feeling was creeping back into her chest.

"We'll come and sit with you after halftime," Lisa said.

"See you later," Ann added.

❄ ❄ ❄

"Did you remember to bring the video?" Lisa asked Ann when they got to Cristina's house. She nodded. "It's so romantic, Cris. You'll love it. I cried and cried." They all piled into Cristina's tiny room while she rummaged in the closet for her pajamas. Bete would have the room to herself tonight while Cristina slept on the family room floor with her guests.

"I love your pencil holder," gushed Lisa, sitting at the desk. It was a hand-painted porcelain jar from Brazil, one of the prize possessions that had weighed down Cristina's carry-on during the trip to Minnesota. "What a neat pen!" The gold pen with a purple soapstone decoration had been Márcia's going-away present.

"Whatever happened with your friends in Brazil?" Lisa asked.

"What do you mean?" Cristina handed her pillow to Ann and motioned Lisa out of the desk chair so she could use it to reach the sleeping bag on the top shelf of the closet.

"You know. That plane crash."

"Oh." Cristina shoved a suitcase of out-of-season clothes off the sleeping bag. "Mr. Almeida is all right. Another man in our church was killed. His kids are grown, though, and I didn't know him." She said it in an offhand manner as if it didn't matter, but it did. It mattered a lot. Brazil was her country and what happened there mattered to her much more than what happened in Connecticut or Alabama, even if she didn't know the person involved. In Brazil, her whole church had mourned together, and the Larsons had been a million miles away in America.

"That's too bad," Lisa said.

"What's this?" Ann picked up a pink, flower-covered volume from the desk. Cristina pulled at the sleeping bag and almost tumbled off the chair.

"'Today I made a complete fool of myself at lunch right in front of the most beautiful brown eyes in the world, next to Vicente's.' Ooh, this is good. Who's Vicente?"

"Who has the beautiful brown eyes?" demanded Lisa. "I'll bet it's Jason Erickson."

"Yep. Jason. That's what it says right here." Ann ran her finger down the page.

"Ooh! Does Jason know?" Lisa teased. "Vicente is that guy in Brazil, isn't he?"

Cristina's hands had turned to ice. "Come on, you guys. Don't read that!" She dropped the sleeping bag and reached for the diary, but Ann held it away from her.

"Read some more," Lisa laughed. She was treating the whole thing like a tremendous joke.

Ann flipped over a few pages. "'He stopped by my locker to-day,'" she read in a voice of exaggerated passion. "'I could almost imagine he is Brazilian, looking into those deep brown eyes. He looked into mine, and I thought for a moment—' Hey!"

Cristina succeeded in tripping over Lisa and getting to the book. She tore it angrily from Ann's hands, ripping a page, and stepping on Ann's foot in the process.

"Ouch, that hurt!" Ann accused.

"I don't care. You have no business reading my private papers." Cristina fumed.

"It didn't have a lock on it," Ann defended herself.

"Good grief, Cris! What are you so mad about?" Lisa made it sound unimportant. "It's not that big of a deal."

"Are you guys done yet?" Bete asked from the doorway. "I want to go to bed."

"We're done." Ann flicked the torn page in her hand onto the desk and turned her back. Lisa picked up the sleeping bag and followed her toward the family room.

Cristina grabbed the torn page, stuffed it into the book and shoved the whole thing under some papers in her bottom drawer. "Don't let anyone else in here tonight, okay?" she whispered to her sister before she followed Lisa.

❄ ❄ ❄

The movie was romantic, and ordinarily Cristina would have enjoyed it very much. Tonight she sat in the back, a little apart from the others and nursed her hurt feelings. She longed to slip the iron cricket from its place by the boots when no one was looking. Tonight it seemed like the only friend she had. But the last thing she needed was for Lisa and Ann to tease her about her "bug."

They had no business reading her diary. That was private. Diaries are always private. They don't need locks and keys; everyone knows it's rude to read other people's mail or diaries. She felt betrayed, not only by Ann but by Lisa as well. How could they do this? It wasn't that they didn't suspect she liked Jason, but to read her private words . . . It would be just like Lisa to blab it all over the school.

She cried harder than anyone at the end of the movie, but her tears had nothing to do with the troubles of Ingrid Bergman and Humphrey Bogart.

Chapter 7

Lisa and Ann were out with the flu. Not that Cristina wanted to sit with them anyway. Not after what they did to her last weekend. With friends like that, she would just as soon sit alone. Except it was so embarrassing to be alone.

Cristina had been in Rum River for three weeks. She recognized several faces from the band and wished she were still a part of it, but no one looked her way or motioned her over. The room reverberated with voices, and the hot smell of grease and the tang of pickles was overwhelming. It was almost as bad as the bus!

She slipped into an empty seat at the nearest table.

"Hi." It was Jason. Cristina couldn't believe she had sat down directly across from him. He must think she was the world's most terrible flirt. She felt the heat rising in her cheeks.

"Hi." Her voice came out in a tight squeak.

Jason's brown eyes glanced around. "Where're Lisa and Ann?"

"Out sick."

Jason nodded. "Derek, too." He took an enormous bite of fishburger. Cristina stared. Even his hands looked strong and muscular. "Hey, this is pretty good."

Cristina nibbled at the little potato things on her tray— "tater tots" the school menu called them. They were crisp and salty. Her brain felt frozen.

"Did you go to the game on Friday?"

Cristina nodded. "Uh-huh." She wished she knew enough about football to talk about it.

"I hear Steve was back on the bass."

Derek must tell him everything. Cristina took a bite of sandwich.

Jason shook his head. "I get you away from air-brain Derek and chatterbox Lisa, and you clam up. Are you always this quiet?"

"Me? Usually I talk too much."

He cocked his eyebrows in a funny way, as if in disbelief, and it made the scar crinkle. "I don't think you said two words when I came to your table for lunch that time."

Cristina silently cursed her pale complexion that blushed so easily. "Yes, I did," she corrected. "Three. 'What's a zit?'" She forced herself to laugh about it because she knew that was what she was supposed to do, but the memory still stung like a paper cut.

Jason's chuckle was friendly, and his smile came as much from the depths of his brown eyes as from the corners of his mouth. Cristina smiled back. Her hands didn't feel as icy as they had a few moments ago. "I felt so stupid."

"No big deal." Jason took another bite of sandwich.

Cristina took a bite of her own.

"So, what do you think of Rum River?" Jason asked.

"Rum River?" she asked between chews.

He looked around the room full of teenagers. "Yeah. I guess it's kind of different from Brazil. What do you think of us?"

She swallowed the bite of fishburger and looked at him, considering her answer. Did he really want to know? He appeared to be sincerely interested in what she thought.

"They're all white, and they speak English. It's so boring!" she confessed.

She looked around the cafeteria, now beginning to empty. "There's that black kid." She pointed him out leaving the lunchroom with a Native American boy. "I don't even know his name. He's already been labeled a druggie because of who he hangs out with. But is he? Or are those the only kids who'll talk to him?"

Jason followed their progress toward the outside doors. He shuffled his feet and shifted uncomfortably.

"Everybody here is the same," Cristina said, "like Grandma's butter cookies made with the same cookie cutter. If you don't at least try to conform, you get labeled. And if your skin is a different color or your eyes are shaped differently, it doesn't even do any good to try. You're already different before you start. My skin is the right color. The only trouble is . . . I'm different inside. I don't fit in, and I don't even know if I want to fit in."

Cristina wadded up her napkin and set it by her tray. She

couldn't believe she had actually said all that. She would never have dreamed of being so frank with Lisa. But then Lisa never asked. Cristina realized with a start that she was still identifying Jason's deep tan as Brazilian and assuming he would understand. He didn't look as though he did very much.

"Don't they have prejudice in Brazil?" He sounded incredulous.

Cristina shut her mouth abruptly. Brazilians were usually a mixture of the races and came in every shade of the palette, but an unspoken hierarchy said, "The lighter the better." She knew very well that one reason for her popularity at school was her yellow hair and fair skin.

"Yes," she admitted. "But that doesn't make it right!"

There was an uncomfortable silence.

"I guess you do know how to talk," he said at last with a wry grin. He popped a tater tot into his mouth.

"I told you. I talk too much."

"No! I like it. You're right; you're different. I like that."

Cristina was forgetting how much he reminded her of Vicente. He was Jason, and she wanted Jason to like her.

Someone came and wiped the empty table beside them, hinting not too subtly that it was time to get ready for the next lunch shift.

Jason looked at his watch. "We'd better go. C'mon. I'll walk you to math."

Evidently he wasn't put off by her outburst.

"Jason," Cristina dared to say as they deposited their trays. "Have you ever been to Korea?"

His eyes were suddenly hard. "Of course not! I'm as American as—" He stopped abruptly, and Cristina knew he was about to say, "as you are," only he remembered just in time that she wasn't. Not really. His eyes softened.

Cristina plunged on. "Half the kids in this school have ancestors from Scandinavia. They all eat meatballs and potato sausage for Christmas and are proud of it. What do Koreans eat?"

Jason gave her that grin again. "How would I know? I'm an Erickson. We eat potato sausage and meatballs."

"Okay. You're part Swedish and part Korean," she went on. "Why can't you enjoy both?"

He didn't answer. Cristina had a feeling she should stop pushing, but she couldn't. "Don't you ever wonder what it's like in Korea? What it would have been like for your mother to grow up there? Does she ever tell you stories?"

"No." He headed for the door, taking long determined strides. It was obvious he didn't want to talk about it.

She had to scramble to keep up. "No what?"

"No, I never wondered." He pushed through the double doors to the corridor. Cristina followed.

"But you must have relatives . . . cousins. It's part of who you are, who your mother is."

He stopped and faced her. "I'm Jason Erickson. I live in Rum River, Minnesota. I play sports, and I hate Chinese food." He started back down the hall. Cristina stayed right beside him. "I don't have any cousins," he added.

Cristina wished she hadn't pushed so hard. Here was

the one person in Rum River who might understand being caught between two worlds, and he would never want to speak to her again.

They walked through the noisy, crowded halls as if they were in separate rooms. He was American but didn't look like the other Americans around him. She looked like them, but wasn't one of them. They stopped by Cristina's locker.

"I never asked her," Jason confessed. "My mother, I mean." He straightened his shoulders slightly. "Maybe I don't want her to be different. Maybe I don't want to be different myself. I just want to be like everybody else. Okay?" He abruptly walked off. Cristina walked to math by herself.

Chapter 8

Cristina spent twenty minutes on scales and arpeggios. Strength and control, she reminded herself. Then she worked through her étude book. After an hour she took out the Bach she was playing for her recital next month. She had practiced an hour and a half every night that week, and now she rubbed the sore muscles of her hands. She hadn't had time to go to the mall with Lisa and Ann even if they'd asked, which they hadn't. She didn't have time to think about the way Jason ignored her in math class. Why should she care anyway? She'd be going back to Brazil in June.

"That's coming wonderfully," Mom said.

Cristina closed the book and doodled a few chords. Something in the progression reminded her of one of the pop songs they played in pep band. She worked it out on the keyboard. Finding the melody was easy enough, but the chords were hard. She tried a couple of possibilities, but it just didn't sound the same. The notes were right, but the piano didn't have the flare of the trumpets, and she missed the drums. Her fingers dribbled and stopped.

"Coming to the game tonight?" Bete asked.

"No time." Cristina got up abruptly from the piano. "I've got too much homework."

❄ ❄ ❄

Cristina clung to the boards of the ice rink. Her skates kept sliding out from under her, and she wished Mom hadn't insisted she come to this crazy skating party. She ought to be home practicing piano.

"It'll be a great way to meet people," Mom had said.

A great way to make a fool of myself, Cristina thought. She shivered in her heavy jacket and was glad she had remembered to wear gloves.

"Hi, Cristina." Cristina looked up from her awkward feet to find Lisa beside her. "C'mon. Hold my hand." Lisa held out her arm.

Cristina was grateful not to be left alone. "I'll fall!" she moaned.

"No, you won't. I'll hold onto you."

Cristina took Lisa's hand and gingerly stepped away from the boards. Jason glided by on his hockey skates, and Cristina watched him slip smoothly in and out of the other skaters.

"Jason's good, isn't he?" Lisa commented. Jason whipped around backward in front of Derek Patterson. The two boys crouched and mirrored one another, practicing feints and blocks. Cristina was awed by their control and ease on the ice. Jason stepped forward around a group of girls, did a few turns and a dramatic hockey stop while he waited for Derek to catch up.

"Just keep your weight over your skates," Lisa explained, "and come with me." Cristina clung to Lisa's arm and tried to follow her instructions.

Ann skated by. There was an opening in the crowd at the end of the ice. Ann turned backward, stretched her arms in front and behind and circled around the end, going incredibly fast. She did a turn thing—too quick for Cristina to see properly—then leaped into the air. Landing gracefully on one foot going backward, she stepped forward to avoid another skater.

"Wow!" Lisa exclaimed. "Ann's jumps have really improved. I think that was a salchow."

Everyone in Minnesota seemed to be at home in this refrigerated pole barn except Cristina. Even Bete was laughing as she made her way around the rink, holding Rita's hand. How could she be having such a good time? A little girl in a pink skating dress dodged through the circling skaters to the open space of the center. She practiced spins one after the other with a persistence that made Cristina dizzy.

"Don't lean forward so much," Lisa said. "Try to stand up straight."

Cristina tried, shuffling and sliding her feet forward. Her upper body wobbled, and she clung to Lisa. Then her feet shot out from under her.

"Whoa!" Lisa flailed the air with her free arm as though swatting a giant Minnesota mosquito. Cristina sat down hard on the ice, and Lisa tumbled on top of her. It didn't hurt as much as she expected.

Lisa came up laughing. "Maybe I can't hold you up!"

"Need help, ladies?" Ice sprayed as Derek Patterson stopped before them.

"Oh, Derek! If you get on one side of Cristina and I get on the other . . ."

Cristina glanced around for Jason. He was circling the far end of the rink. Derek offered his hand, and Cristina took it, struggling to her feet. She tried to brush the snow-like ice from her jeans. They felt damp and cold.

It went better with Derek on one side and Lisa on the other. Cristina concentrated on keeping her weight over her skates and not leaning forward. She stood up straight and let Lisa and Derek pull her over the ice.

"Faster?" asked Lisa. Cristina nodded.

"Hold on tight," said Derek. Cristina's hair whipped out behind her, and her stomach climbed halfway to her throat. All her muscles felt tense with the effort of standing up. It was fun.

Cristina was out of breath when they reached the entrance gate. "I'm tired," she said. "You go on without me."

"Are you sure?" Lisa asked, but in a moment she took Derek's hand and skated off. Cristina followed them with her eyes. Lisa had said her goal for the evening was to skate with a cute boy, and Derek had been at the top of her list.

Ice sprayed in her face as a huge form descended on her. Cristina cowered behind her arms. The form stopped not more than a foot away. "Hi, sweetheart. Haven't you ever seen a hockey stop?"

"Not at that range."

Rob laughed. "Come on. Let's skate."

"I'm tired. I'm just going to rest awhile." Cristina slid awkwardly along the boards toward the gate.

"No, you're not." Rob pulled her toward him, and he was a lot stronger than Lisa. He wrapped an arm around her waist, and her head barely reached his chin. She was pretty sure she wouldn't fall, but she wasn't sure she felt comfortable this close to him.

Lisa swept past, holding Derek Patterson's hand. She gave Cristina a look that said skating with Rob Sundquist was quite an achievement.

"You're doing fine. Just lean on me."

Jason glided past, his strokes keeping time with the music. Cristina wished she were skating with him instead.

Rob's fingers moved up her side. Cristina felt them pressing along the line of her bra.

"I think I could try it on my own now," she suggested, and pulled away.

"I don't mind helping you," Rob insisted. "You don't want to fall."

That was true, and Cristina wasn't certain she could really do it on her own. "How about if we just hold hands?" she suggested.

She managed to keep her balance holding his hand. She could hear Lisa's voice in her head. "He's so popular, Cris!

I mean, Rob Sundquist is a star on the football team and everything. If you were going out with him . . . I mean, wow!"

Cristina pushed aside her suspicions about the Erickson garage door. They were only suspicions, after all, and hadn't she insisted to Jason that it wasn't fair to judge someone you don't really know? I haven't been fair to Rob, she thought. I've never given him a chance.

"Want to get something to drink?" he asked when they arrived back at the gate.

"Sure." Cristina didn't think her legs would carry her around again. "Let me unlace my skates first." She sat on the bench in the lobby and breathed deeply. Her feet were stiff when she freed them from her skates. She slipped off her gloves and tried to thaw her frozen toes between her palms.

If she were home in Brazil she might be spending the weekend with the Almeidas on their grandfather's *fazenda*. The long Brazilian summer would be just beginning, and they would hike through the pasture to the swimming hole. In her mind the shouts from the rink were Vicente and his cousins. They would jump off the high overhang, competing to see who could make the biggest splash. Cristina and Márcia would pretend to ignore the boys, but they would end up climbing the hill and jumping off with them. Maybe she and Vicente would clamber up the rocks. There, they would sit among the ferns, where the trees closed overhead in a kind of secret bower, and the green light flickered on the surface of the water.

Rob's voice interrupted her thoughts. "Here you go. Diet Coke okay?" He handed her a tall paper cup. "That's what most girls seem to order."

"That's fine." Cristina fumbled in her pocket. "What do I owe you?"

"It's on me."

Cristina felt awkward. She wasn't sure what kind of commitment was implied by accepting a Coke from an American boy. "Thanks."

"Hi, Rob. Hi, Cris." One of the cheerleaders turned from a laughing group and flashed a dazzling smile. "Having fun?" The girl had never spoken to her before. Cristina was surprised she knew her name.

"Hey, baby, I'll see you later." Rob gave the girl a thumbs up sign. She laughed and went back to her group.

Three boys pushed through a set of glass doors at one end of the lobby. Cristina recognized Mike McCloud and his friends, including the black boy who had arrived that fall. Rob stared at them and murmured an ugly word Cristina had only read in books. She had heard plenty of Portuguese insults, but the only Americans she knew in Brazil were missionaries and diplomats. None of them would ever use a word like that. It sounded vicious among the bright lights and laughter of the rink. She ought to say something.

"Come on." Rob pulled her arm as she opened her mouth. He jerked his head toward the doors that the boys had just come through. Cristina pushed her skates under the bench with her foot, and followed.

The doors led to a dark corridor that sloped downward to another ice rink. It was warmer here. The rink was cluttered with a couple of hockey goals and some machinery. It looked to Cristina as though it must be undergoing repairs. The only light came through the emergency doors to the parking lot. A smell of tobacco lingered, and in the shadows she noticed a couple. She quickly turned her eyes away.

"Rob, I'm not sure—"

"What's the matter, beautiful?" He tilted his head back to drain his glass and glanced up the ramp. "Those goons won't come back." He dropped his paper cup on the floor.

"I didn't mean—"

He stepped closer. Cristina felt her breath coming faster. She wished she were out on the ice under the bright lights of the rink with Lisa and Derek. She didn't care how much of a fool she made of herself; it would be better than this.

"I'm not going to hurt you." Rob rested his hand on the wall above her head. She could smell the after-shave lotion he used and feel the warmth of his breath. She gulped and took a drink of her soda. The ice clinked in her cup. It sounded so normal.

"I know that." She sipped again. The paper cup formed a barrier between them while she concentrated on slowing her racing heart. The light from the emergency doors cast deep shadows across his face, making it looked rugged and manly. This ought to feel like a scene from a romantic movie, she thought, but it was all wrong.

He pushed her glass gently to one side. The barrier gone,

his face now came close, and he pressed his lips firmly against hers. Cristina didn't move. She hardly breathed. She didn't want to be rude, but what could she do?

He laughed lightly and took the glass from her hand, placing it on the top of the nearby trash container. Then he turned back to her. Cristina's palms were sweating. She wiped them on her jeans and bit her lower lip. She couldn't help herself. She stiffened the moment his hands touched her back.

He stiffened, too. "What's the matter? You aren't thinking of that mongrel hockey player, are you?"

Cristina was confused. "Who?"

"Erickson, the slant-eyed foreigner . . ." Rob went off in a string of obscenities, racial slurs, and accusations. Cristina wasn't afraid anymore. She was angry.

"What kind of idiotic bigot are you?" she demanded. "Jason isn't any of those things. You're just jealous. You're afraid he might turn out to be a better football player than you are. You're afraid you might not be as good as your father, so you have to tear everyone else down." Even in the shadows she could see his eyes gleaming with anger. "You're a coward who sneaks around in the dark and paints obscenities on innocent people's garages."

Rob's eyes narrowed. "What do you know about that?"

"I was there." She stomped her foot and leaned toward him. Rob took one step back. "I helped paint over it the next day," Cristina went on. "You did it, didn't you? I saw the spray paint on your jeans. Jason's mother didn't want anyone to know. She didn't want Jason and Matt to be hurt.

You wanted to get back at Jason for his great plays when you had a bad game, but you didn't. All you hurt was a poor defenseless single mother who never did anything to you. You're disgusting." She turned abruptly to leave.

He hissed an ugly name in her ear. Cristina felt his rough hand on her shoulder, but another shape loomed out of the shadows and lurched at her.

Cristina screamed.

She threw herself against the wall as the attacker hurled past. He crashed hard into Rob and both boys tumbled to the floor, struggling wildly in the semidarkness. They rolled over and over, emitting little grunts and curses.

"Stop it!" Cristina cried. "Stop it this instant!" She reached for them and nearly got an elbow in her face.

The two boys rolled into the square of light from the emergency doors. Rob was on top. The other boy was hampered by the hockey skates he still wore. The light fell on his dark hair and angry face. Cristina felt sick. It was Jason. He must have heard.

"Stop it!" she screamed. "Jason, please stop!" Rob twisted the T-shirt at Jason's throat.

"You're choking him, Rob! Get off!"

Jason gave a hard kick and flipped them both. His fist connected with Rob's cheek.

The doors at the top of the ramp opened, and a man in a nylon rink jacket burst in. "What's going on here?" The lights came on slowly. Curious teenagers crowded in behind the manager.

"Hey! Hey! Enough of that!" He laid a firm hand on Jason's shoulder. "What do you think you're doing down here? I smell the tobacco. Did you bring anything else you shouldn't have?"

Jason scrambled to his feet. His eyes darted from Cristina to the crowd on the ramp to the manager. His hair was tousled and his cheeks flushed and he blinked in the bright light. Rob was breathing hard. A slash gaped in the leg of his jeans, torn by the blade of Jason's skate.

"Do you have an explanation for this?" The manager looked at Jason. Jason glanced at Cristina and hung his head. He shook it slowly. The manager turned to Rob. Rob started to say something but closed his mouth. He must have realized that an explanation would bring out the subject of the argument. Cristina knew he would never admit to vandalizing the Erickson garage.

"A personal disagreement," was all he said.

"Well, you two are out of here." The manager propelled both boys toward the emergency exit.

"I'm still wearing my skates," Jason said.

"Get 'em off." The man crossed his arms and stared until Jason stood in his stocking feet. "Now out. And I don't want to see you back here tonight."

"But our stuff . . ." Rob insisted.

"One of your friends can get it." The manager jerked his head toward the cluster of young people watching silently from the ramp. His tone didn't allow for argument. One of Rob's buddies nodded to him and started up the ramp.

"I'll get your things, Jason," Cristina said. "Where are they?" The words had a pinched sound.

He told her where to find them. "I'll . . . I'll meet you out front."

The students on the ramp stepped back for Cristina to pass. A low murmur followed her, but she didn't meet anyone's eye. If she had been cold on the ice, she was warm enough now. Her cheeks burned.

"Excuse me," she said as she pushed through the doors.

"What's going on?" asked a girl entering from the lobby. Cristina didn't answer.

Lisa and Derek were still talking and laughing at the edge of the ice. Cristina traded her rental skates for her shoes at the window and carried them outside along with Jason's things.

"Thanks." He met her at the steps but didn't look at her as he took his equipment bag from her hand.

Fishing for a pair of athletic shoes, he murmured, "I'm sorry." He looked beyond her, not at her eyes. "Coach gave us this big lecture about 'leadership qualities' and 'team unity.' I just blew my chance of ever being quarterback."

"And Rob didn't?"

His eyes jerked to hers. His face relaxed, almost into a smile.

"You heard what we were saying, didn't you?" she said.

He nodded. "I followed you. I didn't trust Rob."

"I don't trust Rob either. Thanks." She fiddled with her shoelace. "I'm sorry you heard. Your mom said you'd be mad. That's why she didn't want you to know."

He let out his breath in a harsh sigh. "She can't be protecting me all the time." He sat on the steps to put on his shoes. Cristina sat beside him, and they tied their laces in silence.

Jason swore. "I just don't want her to be hurt any more."

Cristina wanted to say something to make it all right, but there wasn't anything she could say.

Jason stuffed his skates in his bag and fumbled with the zipper. "There was something on the news the other night about a famine in North Korea." He gazed straight ahead. "I asked my mom about it. She said she came from the South." He looked at Cristina with a shy smile. "She seemed pleased that I asked."

Cristina laid her hand on the back of his. He turned it over and clasped her fingers. "Until I met you I always thought being different was bad. That's what Rob thinks. Even Lisa."

Cristina studied the athletic bag at their feet.

Jason went on. "Maybe I've been too busy trying to prove I'm American. I never thought there might be something more."

Cristina took a deep breath and let it out slowly. "Maybe I've been too busy trying to prove I'm not American," she admitted. She looked up at him. "I don't know what I am."

Chapter 9

The sky had clouded over when Cristina and Bete got off the bus Monday afternoon. The woods were dark and dreary despite the touches of October red and gold.

When they entered the house, Mom and Dad were seated at the kitchen table with the coffeepot between them. As the girls came into the kitchen, Mom looked up, surprised, and glanced at the clock.

"I guess it is time for you to be home," she said as though she could hardly believe it.

A news magazine, still in its wrapper, was on the table, and a small stack of mail. Only one letter appeared to have been opened, and it lay spread on the table between them.

Cristina got a *demitasse* from the cupboard and headed for the pot. The coffee would be Brazilian—strong and sweet. Mom had brought several kilos with her, hoping they would last the year.

"I'll take some of that." Dad jiggled his tiny painted cup in the teasing way he had. Cristina filled it.

Mom slipped the letter off the table and folded it. She carried her dirty cup to the sink with the letter tucked under her arm, unreadable. Cristina hadn't been the least bit interested in the letter until then. No doubt it was some adult business. Now she wondered exactly what.

The opened envelope lay on the other side of her father, who hadn't moved. It had a printed return address with a fancy logo. "Northland College," Cristina read. She looked at the logo, at her father, and back at the logo.

"What's the matter?" asked Bete. She was as suspicious as Cristina, and looked from one parent to the other. Cristina wasn't at all sure she wanted to know the answer.

"Nothing's the matter." Her mother's voice sounded a trifle too careless. "Why should anything be the matter?"

"You're acting funny." Bete always said exactly what she thought. Her look demanded an answer.

"Carol," said their father, holding out his hand for the letter, "ultimately the girls must be part of any decision. They may as well know now."

"But John, we don't even know what we think yet!"

"They wouldn't be part of the decision if we made up our minds and then told them about it."

Mom couldn't say much to that. She handed over the letter.

Dad smoothed it out in front of him and was quiet for a moment. "I've been invited to head up the missions department at Northland College in St. Cloud," he said at last.

Cristina stared at her untouched *cafezinho*. She didn't at all like the way this sounded. "Where would we live?" she demanded.

"Well," her father answered slowly, "I presume we'd move to St. Cloud. It would be only an hour or so away from Bete if she went to one of the schools in the Twin Cities."

"Maybe you'd even like to look at St. Cloud State for the first couple of years." Mom brightened considerably. Bete was hoping to study mechanical engineering, or Mom might have suggested Northland itself.

"I could save money by living at home, couldn't I?" Bete actually sounded cheerful. Cristina knew Bete wasn't excited at the prospect of being a continent away from the rest of the family next year. But for none of them to go back to Brazil . . . ?

"What about the seminary in Campo Grande?" Cristina blurted out. "You've been telling all the churches how important that is!"

"It is important, Cristina." Her father looked pained by her accusing tone. "But if I took this job, it would be an opportunity to multiply myself—to train more people who'd be able to teach in Campo Grande—and not only there, but in other parts of the world. It's a question of what would be most strategic for the kingdom of God, and what would be best for our family at this time in our lives."

"But what about me?" Cristina's eyes grew wide. "I don't want to live in St. Cloud! I want to go home to Brazil." She stood up abruptly, and her chair clattered to the floor behind her.

Her mother gasped. Her father laid a hand on her arm. "Cristina, calm down. There'd be opportunities to take groups of students to Brazil—and to other places—for field experience and to supervise cross-cultural internships."

How could she calm down when everything was falling apart? "You don't care about me!" she cried. "All you care about is being near Bete!" She was sobbing as she fled the room and dashed into the girls' bedroom. She slammed the door as hard as she could.

How could they do this to her? How could they even consider not going home to the house on *Rua das Garças?* She had lived there most of her life. How could they even think of staying in this cold country where she would always be the odd one out? She threw herself across her bed and pounded the pillow in her frustration.

They wouldn't even stay here in Rum River. If they moved to St. Cloud she would have to start all over making friends. She couldn't hang out with Lisa and Ann. There would probably be a pep band, but she still wouldn't be in it. She didn't know how to play anything except the stupid piano. She would be left out again, and there wouldn't be anyone to say, "Cris can play the bass drum." Not that it made any difference now that Steve's finger was better.

She was whining again; she knew it. But she couldn't help it. All the good-byes she had ever known seemed to have stayed hidden away inside her, fusing together in a giant lump. Now that lump filled her insides and pressed against her heart and lungs so she couldn't breath. She wished she had hidden the iron cricket in her room instead of leaving it by the door. No one would have missed it at this time of year between summer breezes and winter boots. She longed to press the cold iron into her aching gut.

Back home in Brazil the band wouldn't matter. Nobody else played an instrument either, and everyone admired her because she played the piano so well. In Brazil she was always at the center of a lively group, singing and laughing and enjoying themselves. Cristina squeezed her eyes tightly shut and buried her face in the pillow.

She thought of Márcia, who always begged her to play her favorite song . . . and Vicente, strumming his guitar . . . and Bete and the others harmonizing and tapping feet or clapping to the rhythm. Of course, it wouldn't be the same without Bete.

Bete wouldn't be coming home for Christmas or even the summer. It was too far and too expensive. Even phone calls cost a lot. Of course, there was e-mail, but it wouldn't be the same as hearing her sister's voice. That would be the hardest good-bye of all.

The door opened quietly. Cristina could tell by the footsteps that it was her mother who had come in. The bed springs creaked as her mother sat down and began to gently stroke her back. It had been her way of soothing Cristina since she was a baby. Cristina almost expected to hear her begin a favorite lullaby. But her mother was silent. The fingers gently caressed her back, her shoulders, her arms, and moved up her neck and into her hair. Cristina could feel the tension draining out of her body. Her eyes grew moist again.

"You know we do care about you, just as much as we do about Elizabeth," her mother said quietly. Cristina sniffled and said nothing. "It's partly for your sake that we thought this might be a good idea."

"My sake?" Cristina twisted around to stare at her mother.

"Mm hum." Mom's hand paused momentarily on her back. "We know it hasn't been easy for you. We wonder—is it fair to ask you to settle in here this year . . . then uproot you to take you back to Brazil for next year . . . only to turn around and send you back to the States for college the following year? After hearing how you felt just now, Dad suggested that if we do stay, maybe he could commute to St. Cloud next year so that you could finish high school in Rum River."

Cristina turned over and stared at her mother.

"It's a possibility." Her mother's eyes were concerned. "We want to do what's best for the whole family. We want to do what God wants, and we know that will be right for all of us." She brushed a stray strand of yellow hair off Cristina's cheek. "Staying in the States is a completely new idea, Cristina. It hasn't been decided at all. It's something to think about and pray about.

"You know, you aren't the only one who loves Brazil!" she teased. "Do you think I wouldn't miss my breezy veranda, fresh fruits and vegetables all year round, cut flowers every week from the street market, my friends, my English students? There aren't many openings for teachers of English as a second language at Northland College."

It hadn't occurred to Cristina that her mother might have to give up something, too.

"Saying yes to one good thing means saying no to others," her mother said softly. "We have a lot to think about and pray about!"

Cristina flopped back on her stomach. She knew she ought to apologize, but she didn't.

Mom stroked her back in silence for a few more minutes. Cristina heard her sigh when she stood up.

"I still want to go back to Brazil!" she insisted as her mother closed the door.

❋ ❋ ❋

Cristina was left on her own until Bete called her for supper. Her father tried to give her a hug when she came into the room. She accepted the hug but didn't reciprocate. Dinner talk was deliberately cheerful, and covered every topic under the sun except Northland College.

As the girls got ready for bed, Cristina stood in front of the mirror, looking at her reflection and brushing her hair. She tried brushing it all to one side. It looked silly. She brushed it forward over her face. A definite improvement. She parted the tresses and let her nose stick through like those expensive dogs she had seen in magazines. She stuck out her tongue at her reflection.

"My nose is too big," she said. "Unless I smile, there's nothing attractive about me."

"That's not true, and you know it," said Bete.

Cristina sighed and brushed her hair back. She heard her own voice talking to Jason. *It's part of who you are. Why can't you enjoy both? Both America and Brazil?* Brazil would be part of who she was for the rest of her life, even if she never went back. Of course, she would go back. If Mom and Dad refused to take her, she would go on her own when she was grown up. *I was born in Brazil. I'm a Brazilian citizen.*

She jerked the brush through her hair. "Ow!"

Bete looked up from the book she was reading in bed and laughed. "Pulling it out won't help."

Cristina dropped the brush on the dresser. "Why doesn't it bother you like it bothers me?"

Bete furrowed her brow. "Why doesn't what bother me?"

"Missing Brazil . . . and saying good-byes . . . and always having to start over and stuff like that."

Bete shrugged. "We're just different." The reflection of Bete's eyes held Cristina's in the glass. "I don't need as many friends as you do. One or two is enough. Where I am doesn't change who I am."

"Am I vain?" Cristina whirled around to face her sister. "Do I just want to go back to Brazil because I'm popular there, and here I'm a nobody?"

"You're not a nobody here."

Cristina picked up the fingernail polish she bought last weekend. "No, I guess I'm not a nobody here." She plopped on the bed facing her sister. "I'm a weirdo." She crossed her legs and focused on painting her thumbnail.

"You're not a weirdo." Bete laughed. "You're just you—a two-culture kid. You're different—special."

"Weird," Cristina corrected her. She held out her hand to check the effect of the polish.

"Blue?" said Bete. "Now that's weird."

Chapter 10

"These jeans are nice." Cristina admired the cut of the designer jeans that she held up for her mother's inspection. Mom pulled on the seams and examined the stitching. Shopping with her mother was a lot different from shopping with Lisa and Ann. Cristina waited.

Mom turned over the price tag. "The ones on this rack are a lot less expensive." She picked up a pair of the store brand. Cristina sighed. They were almost the same, but lacked the label on the pocket. She didn't say anything.

Mom seemed to read the silence. "Your friends have the other kind, don't they?" She hesitated with the designer brand in one hand and the store brand in the other. Cristina held her breath. "If it's important to you, maybe this once—"

"Could I?" Cristina reached for the designer jeans. "I'll try them on. I'll show you how they fit. They look really good." She couldn't believe her mother would consider spending twice as much just because it was what the other kids wore.

She darted into the changing room and slipped out of

her old jeans. After sliding into the new ones, she turned this way and that in front of the mirror admiring how she looked. The label on the hip pocket had real class. She looked at the price tag again. It was a lot of money for a pair of jeans. In Brazil that money could buy . . . "But we aren't in Brazil," Cristina told herself.

She pushed back the curtain. "See, Mom?"

"They do fit you nicely," Mom admitted. "I suppose if it's really what you want—"

"It is."

Mom smiled. "Okay. Take them off and we'll pay for them."

When Cristina came out of the changing room, clutching the new jeans, she was floating on air. Her mother was examining a dark blue knit dress that looked like something the school librarian might wear.

"This one is lovely," she said. "It would be excellent for speaking at conferences." Cristina let out her breath when she realized the dress was not intended for her. Mom looked at the price tag. "I always knew I had good taste," she said and turned away. "Now what else should we look at?"

"I don't need anything else," Cristina said.

"I didn't ask if you needed anything. You have a birthday coming up."

Cristina took a deep breath. Her eyes wandered to the rack of evening wear. The blue satin glimmered among the darker colors. "Lisa and Ann and I were trying on formals the other day. Wanna see?"

Mom laughed. "I used to do that. Show me what you like."

Cristina laid down the jeans and pulled out the blue satin dress.

"O-oh, Cristina!" Mom's reaction was perfect.

Cristina hesitated. She wasn't sure if she was Brazilian or American. Could she be both? "We were talking . . . I know it won't happen, but . . . if I had a *quinze anos* . . . I mean, white lace wouldn't be practical in Minnesota. Not in November."

"What do you mean, 'It won't happen'?"

"Well, you always said it was too expensive and all."

"Cristina, we said we couldn't rent the *Clube Royale,* but that didn't mean you couldn't have a party. I think it would be a wonderful idea to have a real Brazilian *quinze anos* with your American friends, right here in Rum River."

"Really?"

"Isn't that important to you? Or maybe you'd like to have pizza and videos, like the other girls."

"No. I want a Brazilian party. I just didn't think . . ."

"You didn't think we cared enough? Oh Cristina, your father would be so disappointed if he didn't get to waltz his daughter into adulthood." Cristina wiped her nose on her sleeve. She didn't know why her eyes were watering. "He loves you very much. This satin is exquisite." She looked at the price tag. "I see you have my excellent taste." Cristina's hopes sank. "Don't worry; your grandma is a wonderful seamstress. We'll get her down here to take a look. She can make it for a fraction of that. If you don't mind that it doesn't have the right label—"

"I don't mind." Cristina had always had the best-dressed dolls in Mato Grosso. "It would be kind of special for Grandma to make my *quinze anos* dress. Can we really have a party with fourteen boys and fourteen girls and a cake and dancing and everything?"

"Of course, we can. You and Elizabeth can help me make the *salgadinhos* ahead of time."

"Can we have *coxinhos* and *pasteis* and *kibe?*" Cristina picked up the designer jeans. Somehow they didn't seem as special as they had before. "I'll take these jeans back and get the regular ones. They're just as good."

"Keep the jeans," said Mom. "We'll manage them and a party, too."

❄ ❄ ❄

Cristina and Bete spent hours helping Mom make the special foods for the party. Half a dozen pizzas went into the freezer.

"Pizza?" Lisa demanded when she found out. "That's not Brazilian!"

"Sure it is," Cristina said. "It's every bit as Brazilian as it is American. Every party has it."

"Yeah," said Derek. "Sounds good to me."

Lisa gave him an elbow in the ribs. "What do you know?"

Lisa came over a few afternoons to help. Cristina made sure her diary was well hidden, but Lisa seemed to have forgotten all about it.

"I think it's wonderful your piano teacher is going to bring her string trio to play," said Lisa. She stirred the meat filling that Mom was seasoning to fill the little fried pies called *pasteis*.

"Uh huh." Cristina stuffed softened cracked wheat into the meat grinder with beef and fresh mint leaves for *kibe*. Bete rolled the mixture into tiny balls to be frozen until the big day.

"I think it's so cool that you know all this neat stuff about Brazil," Lisa went on. "This is so-o much more fun than just ordinary parties. You're so lucky."

"Ouch!" Cristina gasped as she caught her finger in the meat grinder. She couldn't believe what Lisa had just said.

Ann helped the afternoon they made *coxinhos*. First, Mom shaped them and stuffed them with seasoned chicken, then the girls rolled them in egg and crumbs. Ann didn't make snide comments about Brazil anymore. She had even organized dancing lessons at lunchtime for anyone who needed help with the waltz. Cristina realized that when she stopped worrying about which one Lisa liked best, she actually enjoyed Ann.

School buzzed with talk of the party. Girls Cristina hardly knew were hinting for invitations. Ann and Lisa were eager to help her sort through the possibilities. Boys were harder to find. Jason and Derek and some of the guys from the pep band agreed to come. Ann had a crush on Steve Byerly, the bass drum player, and Cristina invited him. Bete's friend, Rita, said she would make her brother come. Cristina decided she would have to forgive him for calling her "Amazon woman."

Most of the boys didn't like being told they couldn't wear torn jeans and T-shirts.

"It's a dress-up occasion!" Lisa insisted to Derek. She would have liked them to wear suits or even tuxes like for junior prom. "You can't come grubby like you do to school."

"But no one in Brazil would wear a tux," Cristina said. "Nice slacks, even jeans, with a long-sleeved, white dress shirt is typical. You can even roll up the sleeves." She flicked her hair and turned away. "Mato Grosso is never formal."

If it weren't for Cristina's out-of-town relatives, they never would have come up with fourteen boys. Uncle Mike was the only one who knew how to waltz.

❊ ❊ ❊

Friday after school, Cristina and Bete stayed in town. They would do some shopping, then stay at Grandma's until it was time for the football game. Cristina didn't practice piano quite so much now that she had made up with Lisa and Ann.

The air was crisp, the sky the shade of dark blue that Cristina had thought only existed in Mato Grosso in the dry season. The maples and birches that filled the town flamed with color.

"This is the time of year I miss the most when we're in Brazil," Bete commented as they walked down the street. They both walked in the gutter, rustling the leaves so that her voice could hardly be heard. "We get lots of flowers and warm weather so I don't miss spring or summer. And although I like snow, it gets awfully cold here." She nodded decidedly. "Yes, fall is definitely what I miss most."

Cristina hadn't thought about missing anything in America when she was in Brazil. Now that her sister brought it up, she remembered chilly winter days in Campo Grande that felt like fall in Minnesota. She remembered wanting to do exactly what she was doing now—rustle the leaves and go to a football game. Only there had been no fall colors in Brazil, no trees that shed their leaves, and no football games. Well, at least no American football. There was always *futebol*—"soccer," as the American kids called it. But it wasn't the same thing as the pep band and the cheerleaders and hot apple cider while you watched your friends and classmates, especially number twenty-four, on the football field.

"Bete." She hesitated. "Are Mom and Dad still thinking about Northland College?"

"Dad filled out the papers, but I don't think he's heard anything yet. Would you really be so unhappy to stay? I thought you were having fun with your friends."

Cristina didn't say anything. Minnesota still wasn't

home. Home was Brazil. Having friends here didn't mean she never wanted to see Márcia and Vicente and all the others. She felt so confused.

Bete stopped and gave her a hard look. "Why is it so difficult for you to admit there's anything good about America? I love Brazil. But I also enjoy America. I'm glad that I get both. Nobody else in your class can say that. Not Márcia. Not Lisa. Only you."

"I know. But they've always lived in the same place and known the same kids since they were little. They don't have to say good-byes and start over and make new friends all the time!" She stepped up on the curb. The crunch of leaves was suddenly irritating.

"I like making new friends," Bete insisted. "I don't see why you have to be such a baby!"

They stopped in the Ben Franklin for school supplies. There was plenty of time, so Cristina dawdled over the calendar display. There were so many beautiful ones; she should choose one as a present for Márcia. Nice calendars in Brazil were expensive. Cristina caught herself thinking the second good thing about America in the same afternoon.

"Are you ready?" Bete asked. She had an armload of notebooks, pencils, and even a cross-stitch pattern for Christmas ornaments.

"I didn't get my things yet." Cristina jumped to replace the calendar of rural Northwoods scenes.

"Hurry up. I want to stop at Stallone's and see if that sweater they have will match these pants."

Cristina hustled to find the supplies she wanted. When they had asked Mom if they could stay in town, she had insisted that she needed to get so many things. Now she had trouble remembering them.

"I think that's all," Cristina said five minutes later. Her brow was furrowed with doubt as she glanced at all the shelves.

Bete rolled her eyes. "Maybe I should just meet you at Stallone's."

"No! No, wait. I'm coming." Cristina hated to be left alone. It made her feel like everyone had rejected her.

Between Ben Franklin and the dress shop was Carlsons's Jewelers.

"Oh, Bete, just stop a minute and look in the window."

Bete stopped and stepped closer to the glass. On display were wedding and engagement rings and a locket that looked like an antique.

"Oh, look, Bete. Those earrings right there. Aren't they beautiful?"

They were gold filigree with three graduated pearls hanging from them. The top pearl was tiny and as delicate as the spun gold of the clasp, and each one got a little larger. The effect was very sophisticated and chic.

The sun went behind a cloud, and Bete shivered, turning up her collar. "Um hum. Come on. I'm cold. Let's go to Stallone's."

"No. Please, just a little bit more."

"I'm tired of carrying these bags! Let's go!"

"Wouldn't those earrings be elegant with my blue satin dress?" Cristina continued to gaze into the window. She and Grandma had gone to three fabric shops in St. Paul before they found exactly what Cristina wanted. Even now Grandma might be sewing.

Bete was disgusted. "They're much too sophisticated for you. You aren't that grown up. Good grief, you act like a baby half the time. Besides, they're probably really expensive."

"What do you mean 'baby'? Who's the immature one who frolics in the leaves like a six year old and cries over *Bambi?* " Cristina lashed out. The fact that her mother had also had tears in her eyes was beside the point.

"At least I don't sleep with an iron cricket!" Bete retorted. "Don't think I haven't seen you slip it into your bed at night and then back to the door in the morning. Do you even bother to wash it? It must be filthy. I'll bet your sheets are a mess.

With that Bete stalked off. Cristina knew Bete would never stand for messy sheets. She was very particular. Bete turned abruptly into Stallone's on the corner without looking to see if Cristina followed.

Instead, Cristina walked right past Stallone's without a glance and straight on toward Grandma's. She and Bete had planned to stop at the sub shop for supper, but the gang would be there, and she didn't feel like seeing anyone right now. At the moment, she wasn't sure she would even go to the game. "If I were still in the band," she muttered, "I could glue Bete's picture to the drum. That would be worth hitting!"

Chapter 11

Halloween fell on the Monday before the birthday party. When she was five, Cristina had dressed up as a fairy princess, trailing behind Lady Elizabeth, the gypsy queen. She had never been allowed to ask strangers or even friends for candy before. And what a strange way to ask! "Trick the tree!" she kept saying. It was the fourth house before Bete figured out why the adults were laughing, and taught her to say it right.

Cristina stamped her feet and shivered at the bus stop. No wonder Mom had insisted she wear a coat on that long ago Halloween. It would have been much too cold in Minnesota for leotards and pink netting. Why, today, there were even a few snowflakes whirling around!

In Brazil the Larsons never paid attention to Halloween. For one thing, trick or treat was an American custom that no one else celebrated. For another, it was too close to the Brazilian Day of the Dead. Dad said they couldn't risk candy and dress-ups being mistaken for spirit worship.

Cristina's mind was so full of her own birthday party that it had never occurred to her to dress up this year.

She was surprised at the high school to see teenagers running around in masks and funny hats and clown-painted faces.

"Boo!" a Frankenstein head startled her in front of her locker. "Happy Halloween." Derek pulled off the disgusting rubber headpiece and laughed. "Did I scare you?"

One boy had a fake knife entering one side of his skull and exiting the other. He walked past, talking about the football game that weekend.

Cristina stared. "Now that scares me. Whatever happened to gypsies and pink fairy princesses?" She hung her coat from the hook in her locker.

"Hi, Cristina." A bright red clown-nose flashed on and off in her face. For a moment she wasn't sure who it was. Then she recognized the warm brown eyes above it.

She slammed the locker door with all her strength, and for once it shut on the first try.

"Hi. You look cute!" She laughed at Jason.

"Hey, Erickson!" Rob bumped him roughly from behind. "You should have dressed as Charlie Chan. Then you wouldn't need a mask!" He laughed uproariously and moved off with his friends.

"Don't mind him," Derek said. "He's just jealous."

"What now?" Cristina asked.

"Jim Carlson tore a muscle at the game in Duluth. Coach sent Jason in to quarterback, and Jason threw this incredible pass." Derek drew his arm back and threw an imaginary football down the hall. "Touchdown!" He beat a fanfare on the locker. "You should have been there, Cris! Jason was fantastic!"

Jason tried to look modest, but it was obvious that he felt good about the game. "And I suppose Rob thought he should have gone in as quarterback," Cristina said.

Derek cleared his throat loudly and looked at Jason.

Jason raised his eyebrows in that funny way Cristina liked. "Not only that. It was a play where the quarterback normally passes to Rob—only Rob wasn't open, and he had missed the last two receptions. I threw it to someone else."

"Uh-oh."

"Listen, guys. I gotta run." Derek took off down the hall.

Cristina and Jason walked together. "So, did you paint your garage again this weekend?" Cristina asked.

Jason gave a harsh laugh. "No. That'll probably be next weekend. Coach asked me to practice with the offense this week. It looks like Jim is out for the season."

Cristina couldn't help but feel sorry for Rob. "What's wrong with Rob? I thought he was supposed to be really good. Why is he missing passes?"

Jason shrugged. "He was good last year. He's always been good. I don't know." He kicked a paper wad down the hall. "His crowd is getting into a lot of stuff. He thinks it doesn't affect his game, but . . . As long as he doesn't get caught, it's hard to throw him off the team."

"Getting passed over for quarterback isn't going to make him very happy." Cristina rolled her eyes.

"Rob Sundquist has been throwing spitballs at me since kindergarten. I've learned to ignore him."

"Somehow I don't think Rob likes to be ignored."

❋ ❋ ❋

Thursday morning it started to snow. By midmorning it was coming down in force, and the students were told that school would let out at 11:45. A loud whoop burst from all the classrooms when the announcement was made. The teachers could hardly hear the details about dismissing classes and getting people to the buses.

"And I thought Halloween was wild!" commented Lisa as the girls entered the mad confusion of the hallway. "It's a good thing Dad did that overhaul on the snowmobiles."

Cristina slipped into the seat with Bete and Rita on the crowded bus. "It's so beautiful," Cristina said. Her eyes were fixed on the fluffy white stuff coming down outside.

"This is the only thing that makes being cold worthwhile," admitted Bete. Cristina was glad they had made up their quarrel. Bete had been the one to say sorry first. She always was.

"How much snow are we supposed to get?" Cristina asked.

"This morning the weatherman said a couple of inches, but we already have more than that," replied Rita.

"No school tomorrow!" chanted a couple of junior high boys as they got on the bus.

"Do you suppose it'll snow that much?" Cristina's eyes were wide when she turned to Rita.

Rita shrugged. "If they let us out now, it's because they don't expect it to stop anytime soon. Who knows?"

What if it didn't stop snowing? Cristina had heard her father tell tales of storms when he was a boy. The snow went on and on for days. Snowstorms were exciting adventures when you were reading *The Long Winter* by Laura Ingalls Wilder, or when you were sitting by the fireplace with a cup of hot chocolate and no place to go. But a blizzard was not exciting when you were about to celebrate the most important birthday of your life, with the most wonderful party you could imagine (almost), and you had to have fifteen couples. Even one person getting snowed in would ruin everything!

"What are we going to do on Saturday?" she turned to Bete in concern.

"Oh, it'll stop long before then," Rita assured her.

But it didn't.

Chapter 12

It snowed all that night. By morning the piles of leaves that had been raked, but not yet collected, were covered with a thick blanket. Rakes and skateboards that had been left outside were buried. Pumpkins sitting on doorsteps since Monday night wore little pointed caps of white. Bete laughed when she saw the one outside their door. Cristina didn't feel like laughing.

"Sweetheart, don't look so glum." Dad put an arm around her shoulder. "It's an adventure."

Still the snow kept coming down. The lake outside their door had begun to freeze a couple of weeks ago, but it still wasn't safe for walking. In a few weeks the surface would be dotted with the tiny huts of ice fishermen, but for now a swirling white curtain hid the shore. In fact, nothing was visible more than a few feet from the windows. Occasionally they caught a glimpse of the Bjorks' house next door when the storm let up for a bit, but soon the snow blew in again, and the neighboring cottage would be blotted out once more in a blur of white flakes.

The Bjorks were retired people, and lived alone. Mom

tried to telephone them and discovered that the lines were down. "What if the heat goes off?" she asked.

"They have a fireplace just like we do," Dad reminded her. The concern that wrinkled Mom's face didn't go away. "I'll go check on them," he said. Pushing himself out of the easy chair, he headed for the door.

"If the electricity goes off, we can roast hot dogs in the fireplace," Bete suggested. Cristina thought that was a silly idea.

"We could roast hot dogs even if the electricity doesn't go off," Dad agreed, putting on his coat. "I'll invite the Bjorks to join us."

But the Bjorks didn't join them.

"He was afraid they couldn't get home again," Dad explained when he got back, stomping the snow from his boots. "I guess a few years ago someone up north got lost and froze to death in his own driveway. Missed the house in the snow and died twenty feet from his own back door."

"Oh, dear!" Mom glanced nervously out the window.

"We'll just stay put," Dad reassured her.

"For how long?" wondered Cristina.

The television stayed on most of the day, the regular programming constantly interrupted for storm news. "It just keeps piling up!" said the news commentator, "with no end in sight. This storm has caught the city completely unprepared. City maintenance vehicles were set to do leaf cleanup this weekend, not to plow snow."

"A storm cell has stalled over the area," the weatherman

explained, using satellite maps and all the latest technology. "Warm moist air from the south has hit an arctic air mass coming down from Canada. At the moment neither one is moving, and we can't say when they will begin to do so." He sounded almost gleeful.

"It all means the same thing," groaned Cristina "It's never going to stop snowing in time. And even if it stops, no one will be able to get to the church!"

The television showed cars in the Twin Cities covered by snowdrifts, and power lines in Iowa draped in ice. The reporters followed a doctor going on skis to deliver a baby and interviewed a pharmacist who used snowshoes to get to work because he might be needed. "Not many customers today," he admitted to the camera.

Lists of event cancellations included all school functions in all the school systems in their part of the state. In fact, everything everywhere had been canceled, and the police were telling everyone to stay off the roads.

"Oh, no!" cried Cristina. "That means no football game!"

"You were planning to go?" Bete laughed incredulously.

"Don't you see? It means Jason doesn't get to start as quarterback!" Somehow she didn't think the reprieve would make Rob any happier.

Cristina might have enjoyed the adventure of being snowed in if tomorrow hadn't been Saturday. Instead she roamed the house like a restless animal.

"How about some practicing?" Mom suggested.

"Oh, Mom!" Cristina complained from habit, even as she headed for the piano. Her recital was coming in December. Still, the concentration at the piano took her mind off her worries for a couple of hours.

Bete spent the afternoon at the dining room table arranging photos for a poster of Cristina's first fifteen years.

"Not that one!" cried Cristina. The centerpiece was a topless two-year-old Cristina in sunglasses at the beach.

"I think it's cute," said Mom, looking over her shoulder.

"Not topless!"

"Hmm." Mom sighed. "Better take it out."

Dad sat, working, in a rocking chair by the fire. He had a pile of correspondence in his lap. "If only I had some coffee . . ." He held up his cup and jiggled the saucer until it rattled.

Mom filled it. "You shouldn't be working," she coaxed "The rest of the world is taking the day off."

"Except doctors and pharmacists," Bete corrected her.

Dad chuckled. "It has to be done sometime." He was silent for a while, rereading the closely written Portuguese page in front of him. "You saw this letter from Tércio, didn't you, Carol?"

"The one that came yesterday?"

"Yes. Pastor Jônatas has agreed to come back from Rio to speak at graduation in December. Wish I could hear him. Did you notice that even Mauro is going to graduate? He's finally realized that he has to buckle down and apply himself if he is going to finish school and be a full-time pastor."

Dad shook his head slowly. A far-off look crept into his eyes as he reminisced over the bright but undisciplined student he had been nurturing along for the last four years. "So many gifted people in need of direction and training . . ." he mused.

He loves Brazil as much as I do, Cristina realized. She looked from her father to her mother and wondered if they ever found it difficult to fit in here—in the land where they were born. They weren't anything like Lisa's parents.

The room was quiet except for the classical music on the stereo. Each member of the family was lost in thought.

"Cristina, how about if we mix up the filling for the puff pastry," Mom suggested, putting down her empty cup and rising energetically.

"Okay, I guess."

"It will give us something to do and stop you from moping."

"I'm not moping." But she knew she was.

Mom really seemed to think that the party was going to happen, snow or no snow. She chatted happily about nothing in particular while they chopped parsley, mashed potatoes, and grated onion and carrot. The quiet voices of Dad and Bete could be heard from the other room. By the time the little pastries came out of the oven, Cristina herself could almost believe that it would happen.

"How will Mike and Andrea and the kids get here from Madison?" Mom asked as they roasted their hot dogs that evening.

Cristina nearly dropped her hot dog in the coals. "Without Uncle Mike and David we'll be short two boys!" Her cousin Sandy had moaned on the phone last weekend about the trials of teaching her eleven-year-old brother to waltz. But they had both agreed that an eleven year old was better than not enough boys. "They won't even be able to call!"

"They'll have the interstate highways opened by tomorrow," said Dad, ever the optimist.

"If it stops snowing," Cristina muttered.

❄ ❄ ❄

Saturday morning Cristina knelt on her bed and pushed back the yellow flowered curtain. She had to know if the snow had stopped.

Outside, the world was gray and still. The Bjorks' house could be clearly seen through the dusty white specks that still floated down. Overhead the clouds were dark and forbidding, but they were separated into individual shapes instead of the unbroken, flat grayness that had characterized them since Thursday.

"Happy birthday!" said Bete from her bed. "Has it stopped snowing?"

"Almost."

Bete came to stand beside her. "Time to open my present." She bounced on the bed and held out a small package wrapped in rose brocade paper with a gold seal.

Cristina sat beside her and crossed her legs inside her

flannel nightgown. She slid a fingernail under the seal and carefully loosened the tape. The paper was too pretty to throw away.

"Hurry up!" Bete giggled.

Cristina felt like they were little girls again. This was how sisters were supposed to be. She lifted the lid of the small white box.

"Cotton! Just what I always wanted!" she squealed. It was an old joke. She lifted the cotton out. Under it, nestled the exquisite gold and pearl earrings from the store window.

"Oh, Bete!"

"They weren't as expensive as I thought," said Bete. "And you are growing up."

Cristina jumped off the bed and bounded to the mirror. She held one earring to her ear, shaking back her hair, and twisted her head sideways to admire the look. "Thank you, Bete. Thank you."

Bete laughed. "They'll look better with your blue dress than your nightgown!"

❉ ❉ ❉

A stack of cards sat next to Cristina's plate at breakfast. They had all been delivered before the storm, and Mom had kept them hidden. Cristina read them between bites of caramel rolls, baked specially for her birthday. There was one from Márcia and another from her family. Cristina wished Márcia could be at her party.

"Anyone who shovels snow is released from dish duty," Mom announced as she got up from the table. The girls made a dash for their coats and mittens.

"Put on those snow pants Grandma put in the front closet," Mom ordered. The girls didn't need to be told twice. Fashion was not a consideration today. It didn't matter that the snow pants were secondhand from the thrift store.

Soon Dad was forcing open the front door. They squeezed through the gap he made and laughed as they tumbled into the outside world.

The snow was well over Cristina's knees. Walking felt like wading upstream in a strong current. The fluffy snow sucked at her feet and filled her boots.

"Whoa!" Bete pitched forward. Cristina laughed so hard she nearly lost her balance. Bete lifted her face and it was covered with white powder. She stuck out her tongue and licked her lips. Cristina gathered a handful of snow and shaped a ball. She was laughing so hard when she threw it that it fell well short of her sister.

"You girls get the shovels in the garage and clear a path to the house," Dad directed. "I'll see if I can borrow another from the Bjorks. I'll shovel their door open while I'm at it."

Shoveling that much snow was a lot of work. Cristina soon began to sweat under her heavy clothing.

Mr. Bjork appeared with a snowblower. It sucked in the snow and tossed it to one side. Soon he and Dad had cleared a path between the houses. An hour later Mom appeared at the door with a tray of steaming mugs. When Mr. Bjork shut off the machine, the silence seemed to swell until it filled the whole out-of-doors. The scent of burning fuel followed them.

"Time to give the old boy a rest." Mr. Bjork gave the machine an affectionate pat. "He's been at this a good many years."

"Coffee?" Mom offered.

"You betcha!" He picked up a mug.

"Ahh!" Dad said as he savored his cup.

"When do you think the plows will come?" Cristina sipped the strong sweet coffee and breathed its warm steam. Mom had added just the right amount of hot milk.

"I doubt the plows will get back here for a couple of days," Mr. Bjork said.

"A couple days!" cried Cristina and Bete in one voice.

Mr. Bjork looked up from his mug. "Ya, sure. Might get to Kildare today." He motioned with his head to the stop sign. Its top poked through a drift two hundred yards away. Cristina breathed a little easier. "Then again, it might not."

"Dad, what are we going to do?" Cristina fought rising panic.

Dad rubbed his chin, appearing thoughtful. Vapor from his breath had crystallized in icicles clinging to his mustache and beard. He brushed them away with his glove. "If Mr. Bjork will allow us to use his snowblower," he began thoughtfully, "we could blow a path to Kildare. Then Grandpa and Grandma could come out and meet us."

"If we had a telephone to tell them to come," Bete reminded him.

"And if they plow Kildare in time!" Cristina said. She felt hopeless.

"That's the chance we take," Dad replied. "What do you say, Mr. Bjork?"

Mr. Bjork set his mug on Mom's tray. "Many thanks for the coffee, Mrs. Larson. That hit the spot."

Cristina stomped the snow impatiently from her boots.

"Ya, sure, you can use my snowblower. There's more gas in the garage if you need it. I think I'll go back in the house with Evelyn, if you don't mind, and leave you young people to it."

"Thanks, Mr. Bjork," Cristina called after him.

He waved a hand at her. "You betcha!"

Dad pulled the cord to restart the machine. It made a whirring noise and then it died.

Chapter 13

Dad wedged his foot against the snowblower and pulled hard on the start cord.

"What's the matter with it?" Cristina asked.

"I'm not sure." He tried again. This time the whirring was weaker.

Mr. Bjork stopped halfway to his house and turned back. "Doesn't sound good, does it? Let's see there."

Soon the two men had the cover off and were examining the motor. It smelled like hot oil.

"Uh-oh."

Those were not words Cristina wanted to hear. She looked at the two hundred yards to the stop sign and then at her watch. Maybe if we had till midnight . . .

A new sound vibrated in the distance. Cristina thought at first that it was someone with a snowblower on another road, but the sound came rapidly nearer.

Mr. Bjork looked up from the motor. "Snowmobiles." A glossy black machine burst from the woods with a rider clinging behind the driver. A white wake sprayed on either side as the snowmobile bounded toward them. A second machine followed closely, its driver looking back over one shoulder as though he were being followed. Cristina didn't recognize anyone in their black helmets and padded suits.

The snowmobiles slowed and turned, stopping a few feet away with the three riders looking intently back toward the woods. Three more snowmobiles leaped through the trees. The first driver of the trio shot aggressively from the woods, then stopped abruptly when he came in sight of the Larsons. He hunched menacingly over the controls and revved his motor a few times. His companions stopped behind him. In a moment the driver turned his machine toward the lake and started back toward town. The other snowmobiles with him followed.

Cristina let out her breath slowly as they disappeared.

The driver of the black snowmobile turned off his motor. "Polaris" was written in gold letters on the side.

"Hi," came Jason's voice. He pulled off his helmet and shook out his dark hair. His passenger turned out to be Matt. The third helmet off revealed Derek's blond hair and big grin.

"What was all that about?" asked Cristina.

Jason slid his eyes sideways at his little brother without turning his head. Cristina wished she hadn't asked.

"I think Rob's really mad," Matt said. "He chased us all the way from—"

"Cool it, Matt," Jason said. "Party still on?"

"Of course it is!" said Bete. "We just have to figure out how to get there."

Cristina explained their tentative plans. Jason looked at the snowblower.

"It seems to be broken," said Dad.

Derek turned toward the stop sign that marked the end of the road. "If there were enough of us . . ."

"Lisa sent me to check on you," Jason explained. "The phone lines aren't down all over. I'll go back and fill Lisa in, and she can start calling people to let them know that tonight is on. And we'll pass the word, so anyone who can will come over here and help dig you out."

Cristina was bewildered. "You'd do that for me?"

"No, for a party!" Jason replied flippantly. "Of course, for you, silly. Happy birthday!" He winked at her, and Cristina felt a warmth inside that was more than the exertion of shoveling snow.

"It'll probably be after lunch before we can get back," Jason apologized. Derek looked warily at the woods. There was no sign of the other snowmobiles.

"Will you be all right?" Mr. Larson asked.

"They're long gone," Jason replied. He adjusted his mask, and they were off in a swirl of white and the roar of engines.

It was while the Larsons ate a hurried lunch that the sun broke through the clouds.

"Oh . . . ," Bete let out her breath slowly. Cristina stared in silent awe.

Although from where they sat the sky was still filled with tumbling snow clouds, rays of light came from behind the house. The surface of the snow spread unbroken, brilliant from the window to the far side of the lake. For as far as they could see, no footprint, no deer track, no mark of any kind disturbed the surface—only eternal, unbroken white that glimmered in the newly emerging sun.

There was no way to tell where the shore ended and the ice began, for the drifts had left the slope gentle and continuous. The lacy dark shapes of trees around the shore were etched in white like the little doilies in fancy restaurants. After the darkness and perpetual gray of the last few days, the brilliant white was almost unbearable to look at, but it was a pain that shot to the very soul with joy.

Anything seemed possible, even traveling through two feet of snow to a *festa de quinze anos.*

Looking around at the trays of thawing hors d'oeuvres on the counter, Mom said, "I'd better start baking pizzas and frying these *salgadinhos.*"

"And we'd better get back to clearing the trail," said Dad.

Cristina had hardly gotten into her snow clothes when Jason and Derek reappeared with four more snowmobiles in tow. Each person carried a shovel tucked alongside.

"Lisa's coming as soon as she finishes making the calls," Jason explained. "She called your grandmother, too, in case there was anything she needed to do in town."

Dad leaned on his shovel, thinking and analyzing the work and the workers. "Okay," he said, turning to the crew. "Let's make our first priority a walking path from here to

Kildare Road. If they clear Kildare, we can get someone from town to come out and meet us. If they don't clear Kildare . . . Well, we'll worry about that after we make a path that far."

The whole gang set to work in earnest. Mr. Bjork reappeared. "Looks like too much fun to miss," he said.

Jason organized groups to work together on various sections, and they raced to see who could complete their section the fastest. Whenever a message needed to be carried or a new strategy communicated, Jason tromped back and forth between Dad and the groups of workers like a young sergeant reporting to his captain.

Lisa arrived with Ann clinging behind her.

"It'll be okay." Ann gave Cristina a reassuring hug. "You'll see."

"Isn't it glorious!" Lisa exclaimed.

Cristina looked around her. Sometime in the last hour all the dark clouds had blown away and the sky was a deep blue, like the Atlantic off the Rio beaches. It made her want to soar up into it like a gull on the wing. She felt too joyful to speak and merely nodded her agreement.

Less than twenty feet remained to be shoveled at three o'clock when a plow ground past the end of the road, clearing Kildare. A whoop went up, exuberant as the one when the school closing was announced. The competition between sections turned to a snowball fight in an instant.

Dad and Mr. Bjork stood by, leaning on their shovels and enjoying the laughter—until Bete sneaked up behind

Dad and hit him in the back of the neck with snow. He was after her in a flash, pelting her with snowballs. When her friends tried to defend her, he pelted them as well, and soon he was as deeply involved in the free-for-all as any of the teenagers.

At last he fell, laughing and breathing hard at the feet of his chief assailants, Jason and Cristina. "Have any of you noticed the heap of snow the plow made when it passed the second time?" Cristina looked up, holding a snowball suspended over Dad's head. All eyes turned toward the road.

When the plow had gone through the first time it was on the far side of the road, pushing the heaps of snow in that direction. When it returned on their side of the road, it left a six-foot mound of hard-packed snow blocking their way.

"Oh, no!" Cristina moaned.

"Come on guys! Back to work," the sergeant ordered.

It took another forty-five minutes to finish the last twenty feet and break through the solid wall that separated their little side road from Kildare, but at last victory was theirs. Everyone stood on the top of the huge mound of ice and snow, clinging to one another and sliding off, while Mom took a picture of their rescuers.

"Not that anyone will recognize us in all this gear!" Lisa said with a laugh.

"But the picture will remind us of the wonderful time we had," Bete insisted.

Cristina had one arm around Ann and the other around

Lisa. Jason and Derek made funny faces over their shoulders. She had to admit, Bete was right.

"Hot chocolate in the kitchen!" Mom announced when she finished taking a third shot just to be sure. "You too, Mr. Bjork."

❅ ❅ ❅

"So I'll call your grandparents and tell them to come and get you at six o'clock, right?" Jason reminded himself as they prepared to return to town.

"Right," said Cristina. "They can park on Kildare and honk the horn. It'll take a few trips to get everything to the car."

He nodded and swung his leg over the shovel lashed to the side of his snowmobile. Matt climbed on behind him. "Do they have a van?"

"No."

"It's going to be pretty crowded with all of you and the food." He looked at Dad. "Maybe I should come back and pick up Cris."

"On the snowmobile?" Cristina asked. "Oh, Dad, please!"

"Only with a helmet."

"I'll drop Matt at the church first and bring his helmet."

The younger boy grinned. "You can wear my snowmobile suit, too. It used to be Jason's, and it's kind of big for me."

Jason looked at his watch. "We'd better get going. I've got a lot to do before this big date."

Cristina flushed. "Jason?"

He looked back at her.

"Thanks for everything."

Chapter 14

Cristina fastened Matt's helmet under her chin. "We've got your dress, slip, and shoes in the car," Mom said

"And I put in the curling iron and your makeup," Bete added, "in case we have to do some touch-up."

Jason laughed knowingly. "My mom always complains about 'helmet hair.'"

"Have fun," said Dad. He squeezed Cristina's hand. "We'll see you at the church in half an hour."

Jason grinned. "If you aren't there, I'll backtrack to search the ditches."

Dad laughed. "You two, be careful!"

"We will," Cristina assured him. "It's not that far to town." She felt warm and cozy inside the down-and-nylon suit.

"Come on, birthday girl." Jason revved the engine. His headlight pierced the growing dusk. To be going to her *quinze anos* on a snowmobile behind Jason Erickson—even Márcia didn't have it so good! She swung her leg over the long seat and settled behind him, her stomach quivering with excitement. The seat was hard and cold even through the padded suit.

Jason looked over his shoulder. "Put your arms around me and hold on tight." Cristina did as she was told.

The machine leaped across the back yard, and Cristina's stomach stayed behind. Her head snapped back and then whipped forward, bashing Jason's helmet with her own. She tried to yell an apology, but he seemed to take it as a matter of course. The powerful headlight sliced the deep shadows beside the Bjorks' house and pointed to the lake.

The roar of the motor was only slightly muffled by the helmet. Conversation was impossible. Snow sprayed out on either side of them, catching reflected light from the headlamp. The wind whipped at the nylon of her zippered suit, and Cristina was glad for the wool scarf wrapped around her neck. She clung tightly to Jason's waist as he headed the machine toward a gap in the trees. He slowed as they climbed the bank and entered the woods.

The forest loomed dark around them. Here, the dusk melted into darkness. The headlight swung from side to side as they turned, illuminating only what was directly in front of them. The path was wide enough to navigate comfortably, and here and there it was wide enough to pull over if they met another snowmobile. Oncoming lights would give them plenty of warning. They wound through the woods before emerging into a cornfield. There, the trail followed the edge of the field until it reached a plowed road. Jason eased his Polaris over the mountain left by the plow and onto the surface below.

Cristina heard a distant roar and looked to her right. Three lights were bearing down on them. The headlights wove recklessly from side to side. One climbed the bank partway before whipping back to the road. Jason revved his engine. Was he thinking about racing?

"Which is the closest way to the church?" she yelled in his ear. He motioned with his head toward the oncoming snowmobiles.

"We'll let them pass first."

A deep track angled over the top of the opposite snowbank. Not everyone took the road.

The other snowmobiles came on at full speed. One whipped by with a yell. The driver swerved violently, righted himself, and looked back over his shoulder at them. The other two tore past. All three wore stocking caps instead of helmets. A bottle flew through the air and crashed against the front of Jason's machine. The sound of tinkling glass cut through the roar of engines, and Cristina caught the sharp scent of alcohol.

She felt Jason's shoulders tense. These were the same snowmobiles that followed him this afternoon, Cristina realized. The lead machine turned. The words "Arctic Cat" on its side flared in the lights of the oncoming snowmobiles. The driver started back toward them, swerving to avoid his companions.

Jason didn't wait. His Polaris leapt toward the opposite embankment. Cristina's head flew back. A moment later her helmet crashed against Jason's again. She felt her body sliding backward and gripped his chest in panic. In the time it took for the other three to untangle themselves and change directions, Jason and Cristina were over the top of the bank and shooting across another field.

Rob! Cristina knew he was mad. That bottle was a beer bottle. What would he do when he was drunk? Jason looked over his shoulder. The first snowmobile was just topping the bank.

The Polaris was not new. Jason had obviously taken good care of it, but it didn't have the power of Rob's Arctic Cat. The other snowmobiles had slowed to turn and climb the bank, but now Cristina was sure they were gaining. Every bump pitched her into the air, and each landing was a spine-jarring thump. Her knees gripped as desperately as her arms. It was like riding a bucking horse. Her muscles, already sore from shoveling, screamed for rest.

A section of trees loomed dark against the starlit sky. The trail veered to the right, and tree trunks streaked by their left. The headlight beam bounced from one to another with a flickering motion that made Cristina dizzy. She closed her eyes and concentrated on breathing evenly. She could feel herself sweating despite the cold.

Jason slowed as they entered the woods. Cristina opened her eyes and twisted to look over her shoulder. The Polaris lurched to one side.

Jason shouted something. Cristina thought it might have been "Sit still!" She wanted to apologize, but knew he had other things to think about right now. She had seen what she wanted to see. Rob and the others were no more than fifty yards behind.

Jason took the twisting trail at a faster speed than he had before. A low hanging pine branch brushed Cristina's sleeve, showering her with white powder. She blinked behind her Plexiglas shield but didn't shrink. She wouldn't risk upsetting their balance.

The lights from the other snowmobiles seemed to be getting brighter. When they burst from the trees and raced down a slope, the others were right behind them. The path curved sharply back toward the woods, but Jason shot beyond it. He plunged through a stand of reeds and cattails breaking the snow surface. Opening the throttle, he shot across the open expanse of another lake.

The other snowmobiles followed, the Arctic Cat close behind. Cristina could almost feel the heat of it. Its headlight glared brightly off the back of Jason's helmet.

Something thumped into her back. The thick down padding of her snowmobile suit softened the blow. Whatever it was bounced against the back of the Polaris with a shattering crash—another beer bottle. Cristina's heart pounded in her throat. Her ears rang with the roar of the motors. Her head felt like it was floating away from her body. What would happen if they were caught? They were no longer even on the trail to town.

A light bounced across the snow a few yards to her right. She turned her head slowly and carefully and saw a similar light on the left. The pursuers were spreading out.

Cristina felt a bump and the Polaris lurched forward. She gasped inside her helmet. The Arctic Cat had bumped them. Thump! This time the nudge was more insistent. She could feel Jason's body hard as a rock under her tense grip. Her own trembled with terror. The pounding of her heart battered her ribs. Her mouth was desperately dry.

Jason was forced on a straight course, boxed in by the snowmobiles on either side. The Arctic Cat continued to bump them, more forcefully each time. Headlights glared on the virgin snow that lay in an undulating blanket ahead of them. They were approaching the shore.

The machine to the left pulled up onto the bank. The one to the right was inching ahead. Over Jason's shoulder Cristina could see a particularly large hump of snow. Something must be hidden beneath the thick blanket that had fallen in the last three days. It was directly in front of them. Cristina wanted to shout, but the sound caught in her throat, pushed back by the wind and the clutch of fear that paralyzed her stomach.

"Hang on!" Jason shouted over his shoulder. Cristina didn't think it was possible to hang on any tighter, but she did.

Jason slowed, and Rob rammed them more forcefully than before. Cristina stiffened her neck and braced her helmet in Jason's back. He turned the handle bar sharply toward the snowmobile on the right, and they cut close behind that machine. A spray of snow as high as a sea breaker broke over the driver. For a moment the headlight of the Arctic Cat behind them lit the spray brightly against the dark night. Then there was a sickening crash.

Jason continued banking to the right until the slowing Polaris made a full circle. One snowmobile careened madly along the shore, apparently oblivious to what had happened. Its light faded in the distance. The second stopped sideways a hundred yards away as though the driver were looking back to see what they would do.

The roar of their engine dropped as Jason slowly approached the Arctic Cat. He stopped a few yards away, turned off his engine, and removed his helmet. Cristina relaxed her grip.

"Rob? Are you okay?" Jason called.

There was no answer.

Chapter 15

The Arctic Cat lay on its side near the bank. Its motor still hummed, and the track rotated in the air. A plastic windshield lay several yards away. The headlight arched crazily toward the woods. A fallen tree showed black now that the blanket of covering snow had been torn away.

"Rob?" Jason called again. Only the sound of the damaged snowmobile answered. "Get off. We'd better check on him."

Cristina stood up awkwardly and swung her leg behind her. She sank deeply into the drifted snow and lurched rather than walked a few steps. Her whole body felt stiff now that the constant vibration had stopped.

Jason trudged through the drifts to the snowmobile and turned it off. In the silence Cristina heard the drone of a distant machine. Rob's friend hovered a short distance away as though he wanted to see what would happen. Cristina beckoned with a broad sweep of her arm, but the driver turned and rode off into the night.

"With friends like that . . ." Jason muttered. He surveyed the snow. "There's no one here."

"What do you mean, 'There's no one here'?" Cristina demanded. "Where is he?" She dragged herself to the Arctic Cat. "He has to be here somewhere." She scrutinized the snow in every direction. The brightness of the headlight exaggerated the darkness outside its beam. "We need a flashlight."

Jason tromped back to the Polaris and pulled one from its rear storage compartment. Cristina peered intensely at the illuminated patch as he pointed it to the black trunk of the fallen tree and then slid its beam back and forth on either side of the torn-up snow. Nothing. The beam flashed further ahead, illuminating a disturbance in the snow several yards beyond.

"There!" she called. She plunged through the snow to the spot. Jason was right beside her.

A black leather glove lay on the surface. A boot stuck out at an angle. Jason propped the flashlight in the snow, and he and Cristina began digging frantically. Cristina took in air in short shallow gasps. She steeled her mind against what they might find.

They concentrated their digging where Rob's head should be. It was hard to get any amount of the light powder in her hand at a time. Cristina tossed snow wildly aside, like a dog retrieving a buried bone. Soon they found the back of a navy ski mask.

"Rob! Rob!" Cristina called. He didn't move.

"Free his shoulders so we can get him turned over and he can breathe," Jason ordered.

They turned him slowly, but Rob's shoulder gave in an odd way. He let out a faint moan. Jason eased the ski mask from his face. His hair was damp with sweat and his face was red and flushed. Whether that was from cold or alcohol Cristina couldn't be sure. She brushed the snow from Rob's mouth and nose, noting that his breathing was shallow and rapid. Cristina pushed up the sleeve of his snowmobile suit and felt his pulse. It fluttered like a hummingbird. There was no glove on that hand.

"We've got to keep him dry and warm," Jason said. He shook the snow out of the glove they had found.

"Wait." Cristina pulled the scarf from around her neck. She dried Rob's hand with the warm ends before putting on his glove. Jason brushed away the snow that had gotten down Rob's collar, and Cristina dried his face and hair as best she could. She positioned the ski cap under Rob's head.

"I'm going for help," Jason said "Will you be all right here?"

Cristina pulled in her breath. Alone? What choice did she have? She looked at Rob's still face. They couldn't leave him. Not even for her *quinze anos.*

"Of course, I'll be all right. I just hope he is."

"Yeah." Jason stood up. His face was pale and pinched. "I'll leave you the light. When you hear us coming back, flash it to show where you are."

Cristina picked up the heavy rubber flashlight. "I will." Rob moaned. Cristina bit her lower lip.

"I'll hurry," Jason said.

❄ ❄ ❄

Cristina listened to the sound of the motor fading in the distance. She clicked off the light. "Better save the battery," she said aloud.

The silent night settled around her. For a few moments there was nothing to be heard but the creaking of branches from the woods and the occasional sharp crack of ice on the lake. As her eyes grew accustomed to the darkness, the stars twinkled like a sequined gown above her. She glanced at the illuminated dial of her watch. Six-thirty. Her parents would be wondering where they were.

Rob groaned.

"Rob, Rob." She touched his arm. "It's me, Cristina. How do you feel?"

He mumbled something Cristina didn't catch.

"Rob, wake up!"

Rob opened his eyes. "What happened?"

"You hit a fallen tree and were thrown off."

Rob closed his eyes and moaned. "It hurts."

"What hurts?"

"Everything."

Cristina wasn't surprised. She hoped nothing was broken.

"What did you say happened?" he asked.

"You hit a tree."

"Why would I do that?" His speech was thick. Cristina hoped it was from alcohol rather than a concussion. He didn't seem to remember much.

"You were on a snowmobile."

"Oh." He was silent. Cristina thought that she should keep him talking. That was what you were supposed to do when someone had a concussion, wasn't it?

"Are you warm enough?"

"Huh? I guess so."

Cristina felt only a faint chill through her snowmobile suit. Rob's suit looked at least as warm. "Maybe you should move your arms and legs. Keep the circulation going, you know."

Rob moved his legs slightly, but the effort appeared to be too much. His left arm flopped around, but he cried out when he tried to move his right. "My shoulder! I think it's broken."

Cristina switched on the light. Rob squinted his eyes in the glare. "Maybe I'd better check it." She gently unzipped the top of his snowmobile suit and pulled back the flannel shirt inside. There was no sign of blood, but the skin was red and there was an odd bump where his collarbone should be.

"I hope Jason hurries," Cristina murmured.

"What did you say happened?" Rob asked. Cristina switched the light back off. She explained again about the accident. She didn't dwell on the chase or say right out that it was his own stupid fault.

"Jason's gone for help," Cristina concluded.

"Jason?" Rob seemed a little more coherent.

"Yeah, Jason Erickson. Your friends took off. Jason and I dug you out of the snow."

Rob was silent. Cristina wished she could see his face. "Jason," he said again.

❄ ❄ ❄

Cristina prayed silently for Rob and for Jason. In the darkness and the cold and the desperation of the moment, it was easy to realize how much she depended upon God.

She looked at her watch again. It was after seven. The guests would all be there for the party. Her parents must be frantic. "They'll come soon," she said, as much to reassure herself as Rob.

A faint hum came from the woods. It grew louder. Snowmobiles. Lights flickered through the trees—several of them. They bounced wildly as they wound along the last stretch of trail. The lead machine emerged and headed toward the lake.

"Here they come!" Cristina raised her arm and flicked on the light. She pointed it at the oncoming snowmobiles and waved it around to draw attention. Five machines maneuvered around the fallen tree and came to a stop in a semicircle around Cristina and Rob.

Mr. Connors pulled a large black plastic sled with sides. It had been hastily piled with blankets. "I knew this would be useful in an emergency," he said.

Cristina recognized Jason on his Polaris. The man riding behind him leapt off and bounded through the snow toward her. He pulled off his helmet. "Cristina!"

"Dad!" She stumbled into his embrace.

"How's he doing?" Jason knelt beside Rob.

"Don't let that mongrel touch my son!" A stocky figure leaped off one of the other machines. One sleeve dangled loose. "This is all his fault! They're a bunch of trouble makers!"

Jason stood up. It was hard to back off in the deep snow.

"Settle down, Bob." One of the police officers had a hand on the man's arm.

"Lay off, Dad," Rob mumbled. "This isn't Vietnam." The paramedics had set up some lights, and Rob squinted against the glare, moaning when they strapped him to a board.

Mr. Sundquist kicked his snowmobile. A chunk of ice plopped into the snow. He muttered something about mongrels and foreigners.

"He's not a mongrel, Dad," Rob said in a loud voice. "And he's not a foreigner. He's an American just like you and me."

Chapter 16

Cristina saw a crowd through the glass on either side of the church doors when they pulled up.

"They're here! They're here!" Lisa shouted. She looked elegant in her dark green lace.

"We'll need the kids to file a report tomorrow," the police officer said as he dropped Dad off. "Don't worry about the Sundquist boy. He'll be all right."

Cristina slipped from behind Jason.

"Oh, Cristina, it's so exciting!" Lisa hugged her. "Brrr, it's cold out here! Let's go in. Are you okay? You were so brave staying out there in the snow by yourself and everything. Is Rob okay? If he is, it's only due to you and Jason. He probably doesn't even realize how much he owes you."

"I think he does," said Cristina quietly. She took off her helmet as her friends crowded around. "Bete, where's that curling iron? I look awful."

"You look fine." Jason tousled her hair. He unzipped his snowmobile suit and stepped out in neat jeans and a white dress shirt. "You said this was okay, right? I borrowed the shirt from my dad."

Cristina hoped the others would think her cheeks were only red because of the cold. She grinned. "It'll look even better if you roll up the sleeves."

"Come on, sweetheart." Her mother gave her a hug as she pulled her up the stairs. "Everything is ready for you."

Lisa followed them into the changing room. She chattered while Cristina slipped into the blue satin dress, and Bete fixed her hair. Cristina carefully attached the drop-pearl earrings, smiling her thanks to her sister.

"Open my present now," Lisa insisted. She held out a small box wrapped in the same paper as Bete's gift.

"Something else to wear this evening?" Cristina asked, her eyes dancing.

Lisa didn't say anything.

Cristina knew Lisa would laugh at her if she tried to save the paper. She ripped it deliberately. Inside the tiny box were two necklaces. No, there were two delicate chains, but only one pendant. The gold medallion was in two parts. Together, the message could be read, "The Lord watch between me and thee when we are absent one from another." But the two parts could be separated and each hung on its own chain.

"One for you and one for me," Lisa explained shyly. "To remind us that we'll always be friends, even when you go away." She gave Cristina a hug. Lisa then lifted one of the chains from the box and hung the half medallion around Cristina's neck.

Cristina looked down at the half still in the box. She picked it up and reverently hung it around Lisa's neck.

"Thank you, Lisa."

"Come on," Bete said. "Time for the party!"

❉ ❉ ❉

Cristina's father sat in a wingback chair beside the fire. He motioned Cristina to the seat opposite and invited the others to sit down.

An antique mirror, hanging over the carved mantle, reflected the soft lighting of the room. Red velvet draperies framed the darkness outside, and the buffet tables under the windows were spread with white lace. Baby's breath and ivy twisted around the silver candleholders the church used at wedding receptions. The cake was small, with pink and blue sugar flowers that tumbled from an upper tier. The pizza and *salgadinhos* were almost gone.

As the young people gathered on the floor, the girls slipped out of their shoes and laughed as they lowered themselves in their fancy dresses. Their elders found places around the walls, while Grandma dimmed the lights. Candlelight sparkled in Dad's eyes.

"As I think you all know," he began when everyone was settled, "this is a Brazilian party. It's a custom in Brazil among Christians to ask the pastor to share a challenge with the family and friends who have gathered. Cristina has asked me to share with you this evening."

Cristina felt her cheeks glowing pink when he praised her and told a few funny stories. Then he opened his well-thumbed leather Bible and read from the Epistle to the Hebrews. His voice was rich and deep, and sounded intimate in the firelight. Cristina fingered the medallion that hung from her neck and smiled at Lisa while he read the familiar story of Abraham. He talked about how Abraham had left his home country and gone to a foreign land.

Then he turned to Cristina. "When God called Abraham it meant that his son, Isaac, and grandson, Jacob, would live in tents as well. In the same way, when he called your mother and me, it meant that you and Elizabeth were called too."

Cristina glanced at Bete, leaning on the mantelpiece near her father's shoulder. Her sister looked so tall and slender, her face at peace, content with whatever lay ahead.

Dad went on. "In chapter eleven, verses fifteen and sixteen say, 'If they had been thinking of the country they had left, they would have had opportunity to return. Instead, they were longing for a better country—a heavenly one.'"

Cristina knew in her heart that Brazil wasn't home any more than Rum River. She had known it in her head all along. Only tonight, surrounded by American friends and Brazilian traditions, was it easier to feel it in her heart. She would only truly be at home when she got to heaven. All that longing for permanence was really a longing for God. He was what she wanted more than anything.

She looked at Jason. He leaned forward to catch every one of her father's words. Firelight danced in Lisa's eyes. She fingered the medallion around her neck while she listened.

Ann tilted her head, and candlelight cast a golden halo through her hair.

Cristina would never be quite the same as her friends. She was neither Brazilian nor American. She was something different—something unique that only she could be. That was all right. Whether they stayed in Minnesota or went "home" to Brazil—Cristina chuckled to realize she was still using the "h" word. Whichever it was, it would be okay. She had friends in both places, but only she could be Cristina Larson.

"And now my dear . . ." Dad held out a box wrapped in silver paper and tied with a blue ribbon that matched her dress. "Happy birthday."

It was the size of a shoebox, and Cristina knew exactly what was in it. She had practiced waltzing in them several times before they were wrapped, but the gift from her father was a traditional part of growing up—one she didn't want to omit.

She took the box on her lap and carefully untied the ribbon, knowing that the moment held meaning. Lisa rose up on her knees for a better view. Ann craned her neck. Everyone waited expectantly until Cristina drew out the new black velvet heels with narrow crisscrossed straps.

Lisa blinked in surprise. Cristina smiled conspiratorially at her father as she thrust her old flats under the chair and slipped the heeled shoes onto her feet.

Dad smiled back, and extended his hand in invitation. "May I have the pleasure of this dance?"

Cristina gave her father her hand, and they both stood.

"Guys on that side. Girls over here." Bete organized the other dancers while the musicians moved to their places and tuned their instruments. The adults stayed in their seats to watch.

"Thank you, Daddy," Cristina whispered. She kissed him lightly on the cheek. He kissed her on both in good Brazilian fashion, and stood looking down at her with eyes full of love and pride.

At the first notes of "The Emperor Waltz" by Strauss, her father bowed and took her firmly in his arms. She felt terribly grown-up and overwhelmingly grateful to know that this man, whose opinion she valued more than any other in the world, thought her beautiful tonight. She felt all eyes admiring them as they drifted down between the rows of waiting partners. At the far end of the room they turned back. Her father held his head with pride. He seemed to be showing her off and presenting her as the daughter with whom he was well pleased. He handed her to Jason and bowed to Bete.

Bete stepped happily up to take her place, but Cristina hardly noticed. She could see no one in the room but Jason. His rich brown eyes looked very sober and serious as he took her in his arms and carefully made the steps they had practiced with Ann. She was only vaguely aware of her father and Bete swirling confidently past them.

No one laughed as they separated and took new partners. Jason reached for Bete's hand, while her father turned to Lisa. Cristina found herself smiling shyly at Derek Patterson. Nothing mattered except the dream of beautiful music and the glory of dancing to it at her own *festa de quinze anos.* It wasn't the same as Márcia's party. But then, she wasn't Márcia. It was good to be from Brazil. It was also good to be from America.

Somehow the moment of stepping into the dance was one of stepping into the adult world. It was a moment Cristina knew she would never forget.

Her young cousin David's lips moved as he carefully counted the steps his sister had taught him. He stopped counting long enough to return her smile. Panic showed in his eyes as he lost count and tripped over her foot. It didn't matter; it was time to move to the next partner. David could get his count again as he danced with Sandy.

Too soon, Cristina came to Grandpa at the end of the line. Her father took the last girl's hand, and some of the adults turned to their spouses, joining the swirling crowd of young people. She knew that her father intended to lead her mother to the floor, but she hoped that she would get another chance to dance with him as well. Cristina saw tears in her grandmother's eyes as she sat on a love seat along the side of the room and watched. No doubt she was storing up precious memories of the night that her granddaughter became a young lady.

❋ ❋ ❋

"Hey, Cris, I gotta talk to you." The party was winding down when Steve Byerly crossed the room holding Ann's hand. "Basketball season starts next week. I'm the center. Any chance you could cover for me on the bass drum in pep band?"

Cristina's mouth fell open. "I think I could do that," she managed, "if you gave me some lessons."

"Sure thing." Steve bobbed his head. He reached for the last *coxinho* on the tray. "This was a cool party."

"You bet." Jason polished cake crumbs from his plate and popped them into his mouth. Modern dance music from a CD filled the room.

"Come on. Let's dance." Ann pulled Steve into the center of the room. She looked over her shoulder and gave Cristina a secret smile.

Jason put his plate on the side table and looked at Cristina. "I didn't give you my present yet." He pulled a small box from his pocket. "The red paper's for luck," he explained. "That's a Korean tradition. Or at least, that's what it said in a library book.

Cristina laughed softly.

"So open it."

She unwrapped the shiny red paper and lifted the lid. Inside, under the layer of cotton, was a blown-glass dragon.

"Dragons mean strength in Korea, and you're a strong person—strong enough to show me it's okay to be different from everyone else." He smiled shyly at her. "Rob said I'm

American. He's right. But there's a part of me that came from Korea. I think I want to find out more about that part."

"Thanks, Jason. It's beautiful."

He stepped close. He glanced around the room and Cristina followed his gaze. Everyone was busy laughing, talking, and dancing. She set the tiny dragon in its padded box carefully on the table. Jason's fingers twined with hers. He bent his head and kissed her gently on the lips.

He stepped back and smiled. "Happy birthday, Cristina."

❄ ❄ ❄

That evening when Cristina got home, she put the iron cricket back in its place by the door and left it there. It was enough to know it would always be there, solid and un-changing. She wondered what the Koreans had to say about crickets.

Don't miss LeAnne Hardy's other book, *The Wooden Ox*

CHAPTER 1

"Ow!" Keri rubbed the top of her blonde head where the springy seat had thrown her painfully against the Land Rover's ceiling. Every muscle in her long, skinny body ached from hours of jolting over the gravel road.

"Do it again, Dad!" Seven-year-old Kurt bounced on the seat beside her.

"Please don't!" Mom gave a tight laugh and gripped the dashboard.

The Andersons had been up before dawn to meet the *coluna,* as Mozambicans called the military convoy to Gaza Province. The column of cars and trucks racing across the African countryside stretched as far as Keri could see ahead and behind them. From time to time, they passed a burned-out vehicle at the side of the road—a reminder of what could happen if the Andersons pulled out of line. The *coluna* wouldn't wait while you changed a tire or a fan belt. No one traveled in this part of the country without the *coluna* since the war had spread this far south.

There was not a herdboy in sight nor a sign of a cow or goat. Telephone lines hung in loose strands from poles leaning at odd angles.

"Look, an orange grove!" Keri said.

"Where?" Kurt demanded.

Keri pointed, but even as she did, she realized this wasn't like any orange grove she had ever seen before. Weeds choked the orderly rows. Heavy branches drooped to the ground, and the smell of rotten fruit filled the air.

"There's the farm house," Kurt said as a dark tile roof came into view. His voice faltered with uncertainty.

Keri put her head out the window as they passed and stared back at the building until it disappeared from sight. Most of the roofing was gone, and sunlight poured into deep pink and blue rooms. All the windows and doors had been taken out, leaving jagged holes where even the frames had been hammered away. The walls were scarred with little holes like chicken pox. No one needed to tell Keri they had come from gunfire.

She pulled her head into the car and stared at the back of the seat in front of her. No one said anything. *If I don't talk about it, I won't be afraid,* Keri thought. She crossed her arms and pressed them into her stomach. Dad kept his eyes on the road. Mom sat straight. She was as still as the jostling car would allow. *They aren't afraid,* Keri told herself, *and I'm not afraid either.* Kurt stared at her with eyes as big as mangos. Keri rubbed her nose to brush away the tingle of rotting oranges.

"Not much farther now." Dad broke the silence. "We're almost to the Limpopo River."

The cloud of dust ahead thickened, and the brake lights of the yellow Peugeot in front of them flashed a sudden alert. Dad braked quickly as the *coluna* lurched to a halt at the side of the road. Dust rolled in from behind.

"Close your windows!" Mom ordered, and everyone jumped to obey.

The trucks and jeeps of their escort whipped out of line and careened by. Kurt jerked back when whirling tires spattered pebbles against the glass. A truck swayed past, soldiers clinging to its sides. Most of them looked only a little older than Keri's thirteen years. She wondered if they were afraid.

As the last military vehicle passed, the driver of the yellow Peugeot turned off his car's motor. Dad did the same. In the sudden quiet, they heard the sounds of gunfire.

Keri sat very still. She could taste the dust that had seeped through the window cracks. It tickled her nostrils. Kurt sneezed. Mom fished a handkerchief from the pocket of her denim skirt and handed it to him.

"Please, don't wipe your nose on your arm," she insisted.

As if staying clean matters at a time like this. Keri chewed the nail on her left index finger and slowly exhaled. The heat and stillness of the closed car pressed in on her.

"What if the armed bandits come while the soldiers are all gone?" Kurt asked. The rebel faction in the Mozambican civil war had an official name, but where the Andersons lived in Maputo, people thought they acted more like armed bandits. Kurt's eyes were wide. His fingers gripped the back of Mom's seat until they turned white.

"The bandits are up ahead." Dad's voice was calm, but he didn't move his eyes from the direction of the shooting. Both his hands gripped the steering wheel, his knuckles as pale as Kurt's.

The Wooden Ox (0-8254-2794-0) is available from your favorite bookseller.

Buckle up and hold on for *Jana's Journal* by Jeanette Windle

Sunday, September 15th

I hate Mr. Schneider!

I hate SCA and every person in it and all of California!

No, let's be honest, Jana Thompson! It's me I hate!!!

And to think I woke up this morning laughing at myself for all of last night's dramatics and self-pity. The sky was again a cloudless blue, the waves curling in just right to drag out the surfboards, the sea breeze blowing away Joe Cool and all his problems—and mine. The breakfast buffet up at the villa was outstanding, and Sunday morning worship on the beach with the sea gulls crying to each other overhead and the surf beating the rhythm for Hernan's guitar more than made up for another hour of Mr. Schneider's nasal drone.

Things were just fine, in fact, until the final campfire when Mr. Schneider opened things up for a "sharing time." I hate sharing times—especially with this class! It's bad enough to bare your heart in front of your own close friends or your own youth group who are at least church kids and know how these things are supposed to go. It's ten times worse with all the country club and reform school set eyeing the proceedings as though we were a bunch of monkeys in the zoo. And when Mr. Schneider's in charge, as anyone from our church can testify by experience, you can just figure what's bound to happen!

It wasn't so bad at first. Sandy Larson got to her feet, tossed her piece of kindling into the campfire, and shared in her soft, little Southern accent how much God was teaching her in her leadership role in yearbook. A long pause followed while everyone avoided each other's eyes or stared at the ground between their feet as though scared to death Mr. Schneider was going to call for volunteers army-style. Then one of the new girls stood up to say how much she'd appreciated Mr. Schneider's morning message. (Oh, really! And what class is *she* flunking?)

Another drawn-out silence. At last Amos Lowalsky (now, really, what kind of loving parent would saddle their kid with a name like that?) got up to talk about what God had done in his life through some youth mission work he'd been doing during the summer, a speech I tuned out after the first thirty seconds as I'd already heard it once at youth group. Every ten seconds he'd stop to blow his nose, a display of manly emotion that embarrassed everyone but him.

When he finally sat down, Denise Jenkins made a comment about "geeks" loud enough to send a titter around the circle and earn a stern look from Mr. B. Then came another dead silence. This time it dragged on so long it was painful, and a seagull, thinking from our frozen state that we must be an outcropping of rock or something, dropped down to see if there was anything edible about Danny Mansilla's toes. A hail of pebbles and an outraged squawk eased the tension momentarily. Then people started glancing at their watches, and you could just *feel* everyone willing Mr. Schneider to pray or start another song or *something*! But he just stood there, looking around at us with such a disappointed expression on that long, hangdog face of his I couldn't stand it anymore.

So idiot Jana Thompson did what she always does! I jumped up and said something *very* short. I don't even remember what it was. Something about how great the weekend had been and how I hoped God would teach me to be a more loving person. It broke the ice, at least. An audible sigh of relief went through the crowd as Mr. Schneider said, "Thank you, Jana," then quickly closed with another song and prayer.

I didn't think anything more about it until we were cleaning up to go home. I was hauling my stuff over to the bus when Mr. Schneider beckoned me over and asked if he could have a word with me. My heart was sinking even before he edged me over to a quiet spot. I've never known an adult to ask for a "word" that wasn't the precursor to something distinctly unpleasant!

Why can't I just spit it out? Mr. Schneider sat me down on a bench and informed me that he'd noticed I was always one of the first to speak up every time we have a sharing time. Then he went on to give me this fatherly lecture about how being too quick to share spoils the effect of what you say, and how maybe if I wasn't so quick to jump in, other kids would be more open to share themselves. I shouldn't speak up unless I really had something worth sharing. The worst thing was, I think he was actually trying to be kind!

"You've got one of the more outgoing personalities in our youth group, Jana," he finished, "and I know you enjoy sharing your feelings with the group. But maybe you could just tone it down a bit. We really want to encourage *all* the kids to speak up, not just the same few every time."

I felt just horrible! I was so mortified I wanted to sink into the ground. Sure, I didn't have anything to say much worth hearing. But how could I tell him I was just trying to help? I don't even *like* giving my "testimony," as he always calls it! The only reason I ever speak up at all at these things is because I always feel so sorry for him standing up there with that dejected look on his face, as though we were all letting him—and God—down! And what about Amos and Sandy? *They* always share! Is he giving them the same lecture? Or maybe what they had to say counts as something worth sharing!

Have I really been making such a fool of myself? Is that what everyone's been thinking? I guess I'd always figured the other kids understood what I was doing. Do they really think I've been putting on some super spiritual act?

I feel so utterly humiliated, even more than when I thought Mr. B was going to make me editor. At least then no one saw what a fool I made of myself but me! Sometimes I wish I could just retire from the human race. Maybe dig myself a hole in the ground somewhere and pull it in after me until the world ends. At least then I wouldn't make any more mistakes! Well, Mr. Schneider won't have to worry about *me* bailing him out again. And if he thinks that's going to make the other kids speak up, he's crazy!

Jana's Journal (0-8254-4117-x) is available from your favorite bookseller.